D1540259

Tapestry
OF LIES

Elisabeth

Phil 4:13 ♡

Elizabeth

Tapestry OF LIES

TRACY POPOLIZIO

Published in the United States of America

ISBN-13: 978-1718828490

For Elisabeth

ACKNOWLEDGEMENTS

No words will do justice to the amount of thanks and gratitude I have for everyone who helped me: Nick, for encouraging me to press on and "put the story to bed"; Lexie and Dan, for giving me space to work as well as editing for me and encouraging me through this journey.

I also want to thank Bruce, Sam, Grace, Kelly, Jill, Michelle, Isaac, ACFW CRITS, my author group gals, and Christa, who pointed me in the right direction. A special thank you to Mrs. B, who once again sacrificed hours of her time to edit the manuscript. Mom, I thank you from the bottom of my heart. I so appreciate the time and effort you poured into the book and designing as well. I love you.

The team of Lucy and Ethel Productions deserves a huge thank you for all the technical work. Marlene and Will, once again your talent has shone through in the masterpiece that is the cover.

Thank you so very much, Joe and Elisabeth, for opening your door to me and letting me catch a glimpse into this remarkable life. I am forever changed by it.

Finally, I want to thank my one true God, who through thick and thin held my hand and led me down this path, who picked me up when I couldn't seem to get a foothold and was ready to give up. Thank you.

PROLOGUE

Mr. Archibault pulled open the last drawer in his wife's bureau. She had been living in a locked facility for months now, thanks to the dementia. It took this long for him to finally finish cleaning out the rest of her things in the small bedroom they once shared. His hand touched something smooth, and he pulled out a small jewelry box. He didn't think much of it as he lifted the lid and stared at a photograph long and hard. *Who is that?* he wondered. He turned the photograph over. Four names were written on the back: Rose, Lisi, Ruth, Peter. Jim knew Rose Meyer, longtime best friend and next-door neighbor to his wife, Lisi, but who were the other two people?

Since her illness, forgotten memories began to surface; memories of her childhood, the childhood of a woman he thought he knew. Now, sitting here in the familiar bedroom, Jim realized he had just opened the front page of a special story and wondered how much of his wife's story he knew at all.

CHAPTER 1

January 1945

"No, Papa!" Glass shattered and screams filled the air. One voice overpowered the others. Lisi recognized Sara's voice immediately. "Papa!" One minute Lisi sprawled across the floor of the living room with her family near the radio, and the next she huddled with her mama and two sisters in the foyer of their small but comfortable home waiting for her papa and her brother, Albert, to return. She couldn't breathe. Another shout and something exploded down the road. Lisi jumped. Wrapped in her mama's arms, she burrowed her tiny seven-year-old body. That scream again. "Papa, why?"

"Sara, please, back inside. I will be all right."

"Papa, I won't leave you!"

"Sara, go! Now! Please, leave her alone! She's just a child!"

The front door burst open and Albert practically carried their papa to the couch. His small nine-year-old body somehow held the weight. Lisi saw blood and bones and started to tremble. Sara's voice pierced the night, calling for her papa again. Lisi squeezed her eyes shut to block the sound. It didn't work. Her hands pressed against her ears. The voice still cried out. "Lisi. Lisi." Her body shook.

"Little One, wake up." Someone called to her from far away. She opened her eyes at the sound of her nickname. "Wake up, Little One. You were dreaming."

Lisi blinked and looked around. She recognized the familiar living room furniture. Her mama stood over her, a concerned expression on her face. "Albert?" Her mama had some sort of intuition. She always seemed to know what was troubling her daughter. Lisi shook her head. Lately her dreams had been one of two things — about her brother, Albert, and the day he and her oldest brother, Fritz, left four months ago, or... "Sara?" Lisi nodded. That was the other dream. The night of Kristallnacht six years ago. The night her best friend, Sara Wassermann, watched her papa beaten by a group of young Nazi soldiers. It hadn't even been a year after that when the Wassermanns, along with other Jewish families in town, were rounded up like lost sheep and thrown into trucks. In the next minute they were gone.

Her mama wiped the sweat from Lisi's forehead even though the temperature hovered around twenty degrees and the snow continued to fall. "It's been so long, yet I can't forget that night, Mama. Will I ever see her again?"

"I wish I could tell you. Unfortunately, I don't know what the future holds. I only pray and ask God to give me the strength for each day as it comes. But I pray for the Wassermanns, Tabels, and every other family ripped from their homes."

"I was so scared that night, Mama. I remember you locked the door after Albert brought Papa inside and cleaned up his bloody face. He was so angry. I'd never seen him so mad."

Her mama nodded as tears filled her eyes. Lisi knew why. Her papa had never been the same after that night. With each passing year, he grew angrier and more bitter. Lisi couldn't remember the last time he gave her a hug. She knew it was because of the war. She hated that the war came. When would it end?

She looked out the window. Last night, standing at the same window, her usual watchman's post where she looked out for the army trucks, her family listened to the forbidden radio program. Fortunately, none of the specially equipped trucks drove by, carrying their machine that detected if you had a radio playing. The announcer had said as a result of Hitler's plan to split the Allied army, a huge fight broke out in the Ardennes forest somewhere in Belgium and France. The Allies were countries that formed an alliance together to defeat Germany. The Germans lost almost one hundred thousand soldiers, a devastating number for the Nazi Army. The Allies had lost around ninety thousand. It wasn't looking good for Hitler and his army, although Hitler seemed to think they could recover.

Lisi hoped not. Was that bad? Was it bad she wanted the Allies to win? She wondered what a loss would mean for her country, for her town, and for her family. Would it have been better for them to side with the Nazis and support the Fatherland? She thought back to the fall when Albert and Fritz had been drafted. Peers at school relentlessly insulted her because Albert was drafted and didn't jump at the chance to serve in the Wehrmacht, or Hitler's army, like their brother, Henry. She knew she should have let it roll off her shoulders, but instead of rolling, the insults piled on one after another, making her an immovable brick wall.

While she had learned to ignore the comments, her poor mama struggled as she took most of the abuse. The small town somehow divided itself. People who were supporters treated the non-supporters as if they were the enemy. On top of that, her papa always complained about Hitler and the harm he brought upon the Fatherland. Behind closed doors, he seemed to make his beliefs very clear; Germany was his home, and Hitler was a crazed lunatic. However, because Germany *was* his home, he raised his arm in salute to members of the Nazi army and traveled to the larger cities in order to attend rallies. Lisi began to wonder how much of it was an act. Did her papa actually believe in the cause?

The town seemed tense as well. The politics of the war began to divide neighbor against neighbor and even family member against family member.

Lisi followed the path of a single snowflake as it drifted down and stuck to the window, melting into all of the others. "Mama, why aren't we Nazis?" Oops. She hadn't meant those words to come out, but now that they did, she held her breath waiting for her mama's answer. "And please don't tell me it's something I don't need to worry about. I see it, Mama. I see everyone and everything that's going on. Wouldn't it just be easier for us?"

Her mama took a deep breath. "Lisi, do you remember Derrik Schmidt?" Derrik was the same age as Fritz. Derrik hated her brother since the day Theresa Berger chose Fritz over him.

"I remember Derrik Schmidt. Fritz talked about him in his letter when he had been transferred to the new military training base near Munich. Right?"

"That's right. He was transferred with Fritz to the same base. The two of them worked side by side to make sure the training base could be opened on time."

Lisi had no idea where this was going. "Derrik is the reason we aren't Nazis?"

"Not because of Derrik, but because of what Derrik stands for. I have a letter from Fritz written not long after the transfer. He was afraid of Derrik. The way he talked, the way he thought, what he believed. It's so backwards, Lisi. That's not at all the way God created us to be. Does that make sense?"

Lisi nodded, but she was still confused. Maybe the Jews and other people who had been taken from their homes did something to deserve it. After all, justice had to be served, right? Not every Nazi behaved or thought like Derrik.

Shouts traveled down the road and interrupted the conversation. As Lisi pressed her face against the window it felt cool on her cheek. *Oh great!* The Berger's gigantic pile of manure blocked her view. Mr. Berger owned a large farm that took up the whole end of their dirt road, establishing the boundary for several side streets that emptied onto the road. The fields extended all the way back to woods on the edge of town. The worst thing about being next to the Bergers was that awful pile of animal manure. It may have been theirs, but somehow it seemed to be so much closer to Lisi's house thanks to the small abandoned shed providing its border on the other side. During the summer months, the ever-existing pile emitted an awful stench that made Lisi gag. In the winter it usually froze, for which Lisi was always grateful.

Lisi watched hundreds of tired looking peasants pour into her small town, filling the street. Where did they come from? Why were they coming here? Lisi stared as they trudged by her house, ignoring onlookers who shouted for them to leave. One girl, about her age, supported herself with crutches. She must have sensed eyes on her because she turned her head and made direct eye contact with Lisi. The pain, the sorrow, the fear, all of it spoke to her through the girl's silent, sunken eyes before Lisi pulled back to hide her face. When she peeked again, the girl had already turned her head back. A woman next to her, probably the girl's mama, turned and stared. Lisi noticed a hole where a front tooth once filled. She pressed her hand against the glass in a sort of wave, as a friendly gesture, but the woman only glared back.

"Here they come. I wondered when we would see them."

Lisi had forgotten her mama was still in the room. "Who are they?"

"Refugees. From the east. Their homes, possessions, everything gone. I never expected this many. Look at them. Women and children so young." Gray, wrinkled skin that once held the meat on their bones now crumpled in hills and valleys. "We need to help them." Looking at Lisi, she answered the unspoken question that blared like the sound of a thousand trumpets. "The Soviets."

CHAPTER 2

The Soviets. Bile rose in Lisi's throat as her stomach churned over itself. She had heard what the Soviets were capable of. People in town said it was only a matter of time before they came here and took over. Before Lisi had time to let those fears sink in, her mama interrupted her thoughts again. "Come on, Little One. We need to help these people."

"Help them? Did you see the way that woman looked at me? They don't want our help. They don't want anything to do with us. Why should we help them? If we close the curtains they won't even know we're here."

"Lisi! This isn't like you. These people practically crawled here after losing everything they own, and you want us to turn our backs on them? How can I do that and answer to God with a clear conscience?"

Her mama was right. Deep down she knew God would want her family to welcome these strangers into their home, even give up her bed if needed. Her stomach twisted tighter around itself as she struggled now against the guilt. What kind of person was she? She was better than that, but she couldn't help it. Thoughts of that woman boring her eyes through her were enough to wipe away the guilty feelings for the time being. Still, she wanted to please her mother. "You're right, Mama. We should help them. We will show them that there are still good Germans in the world."

Shocked at the truth of her own words, Lisi waited for another scolding from her mama, but she only nodded. "Very true. I think you are wiser than I give you credit for. Let's show them there are still good Germans." Opening the door, Lisi stopped on the front step and stared. How awful they all looked in their rags and bare feet! She refused to consider what she looked like, in her mismatched hand-me-downs that her mama just stitched for the fourth time. These people were nothing like her.

Her eyes focused on a boy in the center. His strong jawline accentuated his German features, specifically the narrow face and pronounced chin but Lisi would recognize the blonde curls anywhere! "Albert!" The boy turned his head in her direction – along with everyone else nearby. Lisi waved and jumped up and down but when they made eye contact she froze. The brown eyes that stared back were not the bright blue ones that belonged to her brother. It wasn't Albert. She felt her mama put her arm around her as she looked down at the step below. She remembered the day he left.

Albert had no dreams of fighting in the war. He happily stayed in his own small world, between school and cajoling with his friends. He had never embraced the teachings of the Hitler Youth Program. He didn't care about learning how to fight to defend Hitler. Albert's luck ran out on October 18, 1944, when the Volkssturm was formed. This militia had been organized to call up every male between the ages of sixteen and sixty. That was, unless a severe disability prohibited them from fighting, and even then Hitler gave a very small window for excuses. Up until that point life had been tolerable, almost enjoyable, for Lisi with Albert home. He always caught her when her papa's accusations and criticism sent her reeling.

Staring down at the step, Lisi remembered how surprised she felt at seeing Albert sitting so tall in that exact spot. He looked like he did any other day with the exception of one small, yet very large difference. He wore a black armband bordered with a red stripe on the top and bottom. Stitching in the middle formed words and some sort of picture. Lisi couldn't see the picture clearly from far away. Albert stood when she approached him.

"Albert, what are you wearing that costume for?"

"Lisi, I need to go, but I wanted to see you first to say goodbye."

"Don't be silly, Albert. Where are you going?" Lisi's stomach sank like an anchor. She saw the swastika stitched on the armband.

"I have to leave right now for required training. I'm already late but I needed to see you one more time. Take care of Mama." Glancing around quickly he grabbed Lisi and gave her a hard hug. Then he took her hands in his and looked directly into her eyes. "And, Little One, I need you to do one more thing for me. Can you promise me that?"

Lisi thought he was going mad. "What are you talking about? What do you mean you have to leave right now for training? What training? Where are you going? You can't leave me alone. Please. I thought you were against all this. Why are you doing this?" Lisi started to cry.

Albert wrapped his arms around her and held her tight. "Little One, I have to go. I've been drafted and Fritz has been called back up. Now listen to me. This is very important." He paused and hugged her again as people walked by. "Just listen to me and do as I say."

The world was spinning. Fritz too? Lisi tried to pull away to look at his face, but he held her tighter so he could whisper in her ear. "Don't move right now. I need you to listen to me. People are not really who you think they are. Be very careful who you trust. Guard your heart. Do you understand?"

Lisi had nodded. She was frightened now, but she knew exactly what he was talking about. From her brothers she had learned about the Resistance, a group of people in opposition of the war who came together to help fight it. Fritz and Albert had taught her that some people who seem one way might really be something completely different. Before she knew it, he whispered, "I've got to go. I love you." Then he had kissed her cheek and left.

"Come back to us," she remembered whispering, standing in the middle of the road unable to move as she watched her brother leave. She remembered footsteps behind her, so she kept her eyes glued on him. "Heil Hitler." Lisi shivered as her mind replayed Mr. Richter's voice with a few other people from town. All Nazis. She turned her head and nodded to them, trying to muster a polite smile.

As she stood there, she had realized that was the defining moment in her life when it seemed her eyes were opened and she saw her world for what it truly became. She looked around and began to notice things. On the surface, the town looked the same as it always had, but there was something different too. It was as if Lisi had just noticed a tear in the superficial layer of her world. The woven fabric of a beautiful tapestry slowly unraveled, revealing the reality of what the war brought to her town.

First, she saw Mr. Richter's new office filled with patients. From the outside it looked like any other office. The longer she stared, however, the more she really saw it for what it was, the former doctor's office of Mr. Wassermann, Sara's papa. After his brutal beating he had been forced out of a job before being driven away from his home. She turned slowly and saw the uniformed Nazi soldiers down the road as they left the community pool. Flashbacks had played in her mind of days she spent swimming with her friends, Sara and Rose Meyer.

She turned again, but it was more of the same. For the first time that Lisi could remember she had felt like a stranger in the only place she'd ever called home. Every person who walked by seemed to have secrets, a hidden agenda beneath their plastic smiles. She began to question then what had happened to her world? Why was she the only one who noticed the hidden things? And most importantly, why was she the only one bothered?

CHAPTER 3

Lisi wasn't sure exactly how her mama expected to help these people. Her papa would never allow them to stay in their home, nor would he donate any food or clothing to help them. Although he probably would have if Lea still lived home, since she always had a special way with him. Even Rille, her second oldest sister, didn't have the same effect as Lea. Rille always said it was because Lea was his oldest, that he had a "sweet spot" for her, whatever that meant. She wasn't here now, though, and living in a city one hundred kilometers away with Rille wouldn't help. Then again, her papa hadn't been home in weeks. But, as a good Catholic girl, she would do whatever her mama asked of her. And it didn't take any time at all. Lisi wondered if her mama would go against her papa's wishes and invite people in as they entered the crowd already bracing themselves against the cold.

"They're going to the church. Come on, Lisi, let's go find Father Alder and see how we can help."

"Oh, yes, let's go find Father Alder," Lisi muttered under her breath. Although barely audible, her mama heard her.

She stopped, turned around and looked directly down into Lisi's eyes. In a sharp tone she scolded her. "Stop it right now. Father Alder is a man who deserves our great respect. He is doing all he can for our town during these times, and I will not allow you to disrespect him."

"Yes, Mama." Lisi knew better than to even try to begin a conversation about Father Alder right now. Sure, he led the masses and always made himself available, but what else did he really do? He was nothing like Pope Pius XII. Lisi had heard his Vatican Radio program and knew from conversations between her parents that people believed Pope Pius rescued Jews and had been linked in some way to the German Resistance. These last two points couldn't be proven, but Lisi believed they were true. So, what did Father Alder do? He offered public prayer for the country in a very general way, and never verbally pronounced his allegiance to Hitler. However, Lisi had seen him on more than one occasion raise his hand in a Heil Hitler salute when he passed soldiers. Not only that, one time when she and Rose walked home from school she thought she caught a glimpse of Father Alder whispering in an alley with a Nazi soldier. She was pretty sure it was him because, when they made eye contact, he quickly ducked back into the shadows. Later, when Lisi brought it up at home, however, her mother dismissed it. "Little One, you know this town has made it a priority to keep the peace with each other, regardless of our political and religious positions. I'm sure that is what he's doing."

There was no thought about the "what if" of the matter. What if he really was one of them? Would it matter? Would it change her parents' devotion to the church? To have a leader guide you in your religious obligations and duties each week turn out as a supporter to the Nazis was a bit more than Lisi could imagine. But what could she do about it? After all, being a twelve-year old girl had its disadvantages. It's not like she could renounce her religion to her parents.

Her mama always seemed to have a deeper faith than most people Lisi knew. The way she responded when all three of her boys went to war, with a faith in an unseen God that He would protect them, awed Lisi. Why couldn't she see behind the farce Father Alder so gracefully presented?

Rose Meyer stood outside her house next door with her mama and younger sister. Mrs. Hertz stopped to talk to Mrs. Meyer. "What do you think about this, huh? Mama said they won't stay. They'll be gone by tomorrow." Rose huddled next to Lisi more for protection from the cold.

Someone from the crowd shrieked as an object launched through the air knocking down a small child. "Go back where you came from! We don't want you here!"

Horrified, Lisi snuggled closer to Rose for protection, but it wasn't from the weather. "We're on our way to the church to help them. There are an awful lot of them." She had to shout in her friend's ear.

"Too many! Look at them. Most of them don't even have all their teeth. And they all look sickly. I hope I don't catch anything from them."

Lisi stared at her friend. The noise from the crowd seemed to fade into the background like instruments of a band when the performer sang the words. Did she hear her correctly? Maybe she misunderstood. But the look on her best friend's face confirmed she had heard her. She started to confront her when Mrs. Meyer interrupted. "Come on, Rose. We are going too. Get your coat."

CHAPTER 4

The blue spire of St. Kilian loomed up ahead pricking the large, blue sky like a pin to a balloon. Lisi's stomach turned over as the rest of the building presented itself. She placed her hand on her stomach to try to settle her nerves. Funny, she never felt like this on Sunday mornings.

Hordes of people poured through the massive doors. By the time Lisi and her mother made their way inside, they found themselves in the midst of a chaotic, semi-organized, cattle-train situation. In the front of the nave, Father Alder worked tirelessly with a small group of women tending to the needs of the poor.

Lisi couldn't believe how many people there were. Looking around, she noticed all types; old, young, families, couples, lone, stone-faced shells of beings. The ones she noticed most, however, were the girls about her age. She couldn't imagine this happening to her. She scanned every face searching for the girl she saw earlier, but she couldn't help noticing all the other young people standing there helplessly.

She marveled at the lack of emotion on their faces. Some cried, mostly the young children or the women who had been separated from their husbands or families, but the majority of the faces looked like granite statues, unable to smile or make one movement for fear of cracking the entire stone. She wondered if any of this made an impact on Rose. Judging from the amount of times her friend washed her hands, Lisi figured the only influence it made would most likely be on her personal hygiene.

Approaching the front, they practically tripped over a group huddled on the floor. Lisi's mama apologized and made sure everyone was all right. Lisi, however, did not say a word but instead stared into the skinny, fearful, freckled face of the girl on the street. Beside her sat a boy, also about her age, who looked up at her. Lisi didn't see the fear and lack of emotion in his face like the others. Instead, his eyes held an anger and bitterness that almost seemed to be the energy that kept him going. Both brother and sister had blonde hair and, even though they huddled together under a blanket, she could tell they were both very skinny. Lisi glanced down, trying to avoid any more eye contact, but that was a mistake. The blanket slipped off the girl's shoulder revealing several dark bruises along her upper arm. Unable to hold it in, Lisi let out a small, involuntary gasp. The family heard her, and the blonde brother looked ready for a fight. Just then Lisi turned away but not before she caught his sister pulling him back down to whisper in his ear. When the boy replied, Lisi couldn't understand anything other than the word "Ruth."

For some reason this small gesture upset Lisi more than anything else that day. Watching the family made the pain of missing her brothers, especially Albert, feel raw. Will Albert come home soon if Hitler can't recover? Feelings of hopefulness began to rise up, but one look around her and those feelings sank right back down. Lisi felt like she stepped into some sort of alternate state, one she couldn't wait to escape. Unfortunately, before she did, the boy caught her eyes and gave her a long, cold stare. When his sister looked up at her, Lisi offered a small resemblance of a smile before quickly rejoining her mama.

"Little One, come here." Lisi grasped the outstretched, waiting hand of her mama, determined to focus her attention on what was being said. "Lisi, Father Alder could desperately use our help."

"Hello, Lisi. Thank you for offering your help. It is a great thing you're doing."

Lisi took in the handsome features of the tall man standing before her and nodded. Dark hair glittered with streaks of gray was slicked back away from his high forehead. His square chin and long nose were his two most prominent features. But to Lisi, the scariest feature was the double row of completely straight, bright white teeth that gleamed at her when he smiled. Like now.

"If you both could join the women along the wall over there. They are organizing ways to gather enough blankets and food for our new friends." Father Alder's gaze never left Lisi's as he pointed to his left where the Meyers had already begun their work. "Be careful," he whispered after her mama left. "It can be dangerous!" With one final glowering smile, Father Alder winked at her and turned back to the group.

"God, please help me now. I don't want to be here at all. I don't want to help these people, even if I should. Maybe Rose was right." Lisi whispered these words while she stared after Father Alder with suspicious eyes.

CHAPTER 5

Lisi stretched her back for the tenth time in the last five minutes as she warmed her hands over the small heater in her living room. She reflected on the last six hours and hummed a sad tune. When was the last time she'd worked so hard? Her back was stiff and her feet ached, but why should she complain? She had shoes, though worn thin. Still, they covered her feet. She didn't have to worry about frostbite. And she had a coat for cold weather. The people she met today did not even have these.

Piles of blankets and pillows seemed to pour out of the woodwork of the church as many other mamas and their daughters helped too. Lisi recognized at least ten girls from her grade, and even a few boys, though they didn't talk to her. She spent most of the time handing out blankets and freshly made soup.

She looked down at her feet and thought again about the refugees. Slowly, so she wouldn't make any noise, Lisi crept to the front door. She knew her mama wouldn't like this, but somehow it didn't matter as much as what she was about to do next. The door handle didn't make a sound as she silently turned it and pulled the door open without one creak. Good. She tiptoed outside and stood on the front step. Packed snow felt cold beneath her thin layer of socks. She started to shiver but stayed in her place. She needed to know how they felt. Her fingers had just gripped the sock to pull it off so she could dip her toe in the snow, when she heard a sound behind her.

"Little One, Mrs. Meyer and I are going to...." Lisi shoved her sock back on, ran inside and shut the door. Her mama stood in the doorway to the kitchen. "What on earth were you doing out there? You'll catch frostbite without your coat and boots on."

Lisi didn't know what to say so she stood, staring at her mama. Slowly small tears welled in her eyes and slid down her cheeks. She stepped into her mama's open arms. Her mama always knew when Lisi needed a hug. The tears pooled and melted into her mama's sweater. She didn't even know why she was crying.

"There, there, Little One. I know." Did her mama really know? How could she when Lisi didn't even know? She felt a teardrop land on her forehead. Was her mama crying too? Her mama sniffed. "It's been a very emotional day. Maybe you should stay here. Are you all right staying by yourself? Would you like me to see if Rose can come over? You could keep each other company. I'll be back before dark."

Was that why she was crying? Was she just 'emotional'? "Mama, where will they all sleep? And what if there are more? Where will they go? Will they sleep here?"

"I'm afraid not. You know how Papa is, and we already spoke about it last year anticipating this might happen. He told me I can help in any way, but not that."

Lisi felt her tears rescind. She knew her papa would say that, and she should be used to it by now. Up until today she had felt the same way he did. However, that changed after seeing them in the church today.

All three of her brothers had a sense of purpose, of duty. She often wondered what her role was in this war. Her desire to search for her purpose started last summer when she caught Fritz and Albert in a secret meeting. She had been stationed at the window on guard while the radio played, when she noticed a shadow advance across the front yard. At first, she was terrified, until she recognized it. It was Fritz, her stepbrother. Curious, she watched as he passed the house. She expected him to come in the side door off the kitchen. When he didn't, she crept to the kitchen and peeked through the blackout shades to see where he went.

Surprisingly, he stopped at the manure pile. She remembered thinking what a strange thing to do, but then he unlatched the door of the shed and slid inside. Making an emergency excuse to her parents, Lisi waited for her mama to cover the window and she slipped into the kitchen, as if she was headed for the bathroom. After waiting a few minutes to make sure nobody followed her, she silently opened the kitchen door and snuck out, pulled by an imaginary cord.

Opening the shed door slowly, Lisi just had to crack it before she saw her stepbrother hunched over a table with his back to her. She started to speak when she lost her balance and, without thinking, grabbed onto the door for support. Giving in to her weight, the door swung wide and she found herself flat on her back staring up at Fritz's startled face.

"Lisi, what are you doing here?" It had been a logical question, but one that she really couldn't answer. Why was she there?

Fritz had been angry with her, but that night she had been given the opportunity to hold a war secret in her heart. In her defense she had thrown Fritz's question back to him. "All right, I'll tell you, but only because if I tell you, you need to promise you won't say anything to Mama or anyone about seeing me here. Do you promise? Not a word."

After she had promised, Lisi clung to every word Fritz told her that night about his new work as she sat on an upside-down bucket. "You remember how I was transferred to the military training camp before the start of the war, right?" Yes, she had remembered. "Well, I saw things. I can't go into details, but I can tell you I saw the Wassermanns. And more recently the Tabels." Tears had filled Lisi's eyes at the mention of her two friends, and even now thinking about it again she felt her eyes burn.

"I know this may be hard for you to understand," he had said. "As you know, I've never been for this war. And seeing that my papa is French, not German, I felt confused and torn. But knowing that Mama doesn't support Hitler either made it much easier for me."

Lisi had been so confused. She had no idea what Fritz was talking about, but she didn't want to interrupt him, afraid he might stop talking. "Don't worry, when I'm finished, you'll understand. Anyway, a truckload of people all from our town arrived one morning."

Lisi remembered the morning. She was eight years old. Rille moved to live with Lea in Wurzburg a few months before. Loud trucks packed with soldiers roared into town. They rounded up all the Jewish families that remained. Lisi only saw small parts of it because her papa had ordered everyone to sit in the kitchen so they couldn't see. It seemed like hours passed until the last truck left town. Her mama cried, and she didn't understand why until she learned many of their friends, including the Wassermanns, had been taken away.

Fritz's voice cracked with emotion. "My stomach dropped when I saw them start to unload. They said there were many trucks, all sent to different camps. I don't know why it happened that the one truck from my town arrived at the same camp where I was stationed. Maybe it was an act of God. Who knows? But it happened. As they unloaded the people, I knew I needed to do something to help them.

"They called them work camps, but they are not good places," Fritz had told her. "Bad things happen there. People are tortured and many people die. I knew I had to get the prisoners to a better location. I met with another soldier who drove the trucks. We met in training, and I knew I could trust him. We came up with a plan to sneak the families from our town back into the truck on his next ride out and he would take them someplace in the country where they would be safe."

Lisi's first reaction when she found out about her stepbrother and his involvement with the Resistance was not fear. It was admiration, awed by his passion and courage. She had heard about the Resistance, a group of people who secretly opposed Hitler and helped people, including Jews. Everything she learned was bad, and anyone who worked with them was to be turned in. She couldn't turn Fritz in!

He had more to tell her. "Unfortunately, another soldier, Derrik Schmidt, overheard our conversation." *Derrik, the true picture of a Nazi inside and out,* Lisi remembered her mama's words about Derrik from earlier. "He heard the plan and threatened to turn us in. Fortunately for me, during our early days at the camp, I saved his life during a drill, so he owed me. He knew he couldn't kill me, but he could bang me up pretty good." Fritz held out his foot as proof. Lisi had never asked Fritz about his injuries. He only claimed it was a bad accident at the camp.

She asked one question. "Why are you here tonight?"

"Sometimes too much information does more harm than good. You will know only what you need to know." Fritz had looked so old in the dim glow of the kerosene lantern that dangled from a hook in the ceiling. Lisi realized she didn't really know him anymore. He had changed a lot. So had she, and now with the new information he revealed to her that night she looked at him through clearer eyes. The threads had disappeared, and her brother's image was perfectly solid and clear. He was brave. He was strong. He stood up for what he believed was right.

In answer to her question the door of the shed had opened and Albert walked in with Karl Berger. She had been surprised at Albert, but she couldn't believe it was Karl. His parents were strict Nazis. Lisi had wondered if Karl's parents would turn him in if they ever found out his participation. She finally realized why Fritz was there. She had stumbled upon a secret meeting that night, one that had been protected by a pile of manure. And her stepbrother trusted her enough to include her. She often wondered about Henry too. Was he part of this and that was why he joined the war voluntarily?

CHAPTER 6

That was last summer, but Lisi still hadn't found her purpose. She felt the longing again in September, when Albert and Fritz were drafted. The first time she saw the truth in that little tear hidden behind the tapestry of Hitler's world. After that day she became almost obsessed with how she could help, while most of her friends and classmates easily adapted to the changes. To them this was life, and you dealt with it.

Thinking about it now, maybe her job, her purpose, was to help these refugees. Lisi smiled through her dried tears as she thought about it. Help the refugees. Refugee. What a strange word. Lisi didn't really know what it meant, but she knew who they were. And most importantly, she knew they needed help.

It's funny how life works. Only a little while ago she wished the refugees would go away and find somewhere else to live. But that was before she helped them and met some of them. Now she realized she didn't want them to leave. She wished some of them could even stay in her house.

"Mama, was Papa like this before the war? I mean before Hitler and the Nazis started to take over the country. I have different memories of him. He was nicer. Were those only dreams?"

Mrs. Hertz sighed, and for an instant Lisi wished she hadn't asked. Suddenly, her lips turned upwards, and her mama smiled as she shook her head. "You're right when you say he was different before the war began. He was very different. You might not remember, but when the war began, your papa and I were very much in love. For some reason his past hadn't caught up to him yet."

Lisi could almost see the happy memories in her mama's eyes. "Lisi, your papa has had a tough life. Growing up as the eldest of seven children, his parents expected a lot from him. He had to grow up early and quickly, especially when his sister became very ill and required care around the clock. He was once a kind and gentle man who made me laugh." Lisi couldn't imagine that.

"I guess he was always a little rough. Then came the first war, now Hitler and this war." A frown replaced the smile, and Lisi wondered at the memories haunting her mother. "And he isn't even fighting in this one. Regardless, we have no right to judge him. He is a decent man, a hard worker and a good provider. Enough with the questions." Wrapping both her hands gently around Lisi's cheeks, her mama kissed her on the forehead. Lisi could tell her mama's words were for herself as much as for Lisi.

"You might not remember, but even before the war started things began to change, not just in our home, but around our town. It seemed as if overnight the winds of change swept through our small community. Families that were once friends stopped talking. When neighbors passed each other on the street, a slight nod and a Heil Hitler salute sufficed. It became obvious who the more enthusiastic Nazi followers were when families began to cross the street to avoid not only the Jews but the Jewish sympathizers as well. Flags that bore the Nazi swastika proudly hung outside more homes and were displayed above shops and professional offices of former Jewish owners. That was when I began to read the Bible my mama gave me."

"I don't ever remember your Bible not being open on the small desk in the living room."

"That's because I feel if I close it, my faith will be shut off and darkened like the pages when the cover closes."

"You told me once that the words inside were the only thing that could save me. 'They were my lifeline', you said. You told me that you believed darker times were coming, and if we wanted to survive Hitler then we needed to hold on to the words of truth. That's what you said, Mama."

Her mama was pleased she remembered. With a sad voice she replied, "It's so true. You girls were easier to reach, but every chance I could get I would read to Fritz, Henry and Albert too. Until, well, anyway."

She didn't need to finish. Lisi knew what she meant. Until the war came and took her sons away from her. "I thought the darker times you talked about were when the war began. But it seems as if each year, each month, each day has gotten darker and darker."

"You are not wrong, Little One. However, God also promises us that if we hold onto the Word of Truth, whatever happens He will help us. The Bible tells us there are seasons in life." She picked up her Bible and turned to the Old Testament. "To everything there is a season, a time for every purpose under heaven." She continued reading. "A time of war, and a time of peace."

"I like that, Mama. What does it mean?"

"It is believed that the author of this book of Ecclesiastes was King Solomon, the wisest, most powerful king of Israel. His riches and power came only from God. He acquired his fortune because he gained wisdom by seeking God. He realized the only way to be truly happy in life is found in God. God gives meaning to life, and God created seasons in life. The tough seasons in our lives, let's say, our winter, help us to grow in our faith. But then the snow melts, the flowers bloom, the fruit begins to grow, and we find we are in the sunshine of spring and summer.

"God has allowed our country to go through an extended winter. But it can't last forever. I believe spring will be here soon, and with it, a new beginning. We have to hold on to this, Lisi. For if we don't our winters will grow longer and longer, and the springs and summers of life will become shorter and shorter. Does that make sense?" Lisi nodded thoughtfully. She waited for her mama to say more. After a minute of silence, her mama continued. "I remember the first night I really saw it was the night we heard on the radio about Herschel Grynszpan." Lisi remembered bits and pieces about the incident, mainly something about a Polish boy who murdered a German after the Nazis took his family. It was also the same night when Sara's papa was tortured. "That night your papa refused to pray with us. In fact, he stopped acknowledging God as a real God after that night."

Lisi always wondered when her papa stopped believing in God. Her mama continued. "That night took the last good breath from your papa's soul. I slowly watched the changes as Hitler gained more and more power. But that night, when your papa explained to me what happened while he was outside, how the Nazi soldiers attacked him for trying to help his friend, I knew I'd lost him. Something snapped inside him. I prayed to God every night afterward, and I still do, that someday He would bring him back to me." Lisi watched as one tear made a path down her mama's cheek. "I know there is still good in him, but this war has made him crazy. Even now I see him changing. I don't know who he is anymore. Sometimes I'm glad he is away for weeks at a time, even though I have no idea if he's safe." She looked to Lisi and covered her mouth with her hand. "Oh, I think I've said too much. Come." She turned to leave the room.

Lisi had one more question to ask but wasn't sure she could do it. "You said you were in love, but if he was like this after the first war, why did you marry him?" Her mama froze in place unable to move. Might as well keep going, Lisi thought. She had gone this far. "Did he ever love you? Did he love his girlfriends, too?"

The last two questions were a whispered breath, but they didn't escape her mama's ears. One look at her face and Lisi felt like Albert must have felt all those times his older brother, Henry, won their brotherly fights. The difference was that after a minute Albert laughed again, ready for more. Lisi, however, wanted to crawl into one of the holes in the floorboards and stay there forever. Why had she opened her mouth? When would she learn to keep her mouth shut? Now she had to undo what she'd just created, but how?

Before Lisi could utter an apology, her papa walked through the front door. He missed dinner, so Mrs. Hertz wiped her face and took a deep breath as she headed to the kitchen, walking past her daughter without a word or a glance. The next thing she knew, Lisi stood alone in the living room. She ran upstairs and locked herself in her room. Sliding down the door she drew her knees to her chest and hugged her legs. She felt embarrassed and angry, but as she sat there thinking she began to feel angrier. Angry at herself for ever opening her big mouth, angry at her absent papa for making her mama miserable, and even angry at her mama for acting like dirt under his boots and never standing up to him. "I haven't left You out, either." She lifted her eyes to the ceiling. "Why have You let this stupid war go on for so long? And why haven't You killed Adolf Hitler yet? If you had, my brothers would be able to come home and Papa would be nice to us again." She kept her eyes lifted, waiting for a reply, but she knew she wouldn't get one. Even though her mama still believed, right now it felt like God had stopped listening to her family long ago.

CHAPTER 7

"**I** prohibit this family from opening my door to strangers. What if they're Reds, Anika? Are you willing to risk your daughter's life? Maybe you don't care, but I do."

Sure, he cared about her as much as he cared about the Berger's manure pile. Lisi held her breath and closed her eyes. More refugees arrived today. "Mama, why do you let him do that to you?" Her whispered words evaporated into the air as soon as she spoke them like steam from a boiling kettle. "Why do you let him make you out to look like the bad guy so he can play the role of a saint?" If her papa ever helped anyone, there was always something in it for him.

"Of course I don't want to put Lisi's life in danger any more than I want to put yours or mine. But these people, Otto. They're German, just like you and me. They aren't Reds. If you just saw them you'd understand. They have nothing, just the clothes on their backs. How can we refuse to give them a warm place to sleep, especially now that we have three open beds?"

"You don't see it. I do. Prisoners of war and refugees have been breaking into small town homes. They steal whatever they can find. Sometimes they hurt the homeowners. Absolutely not! End of discussion! Now, I will walk down to the church with you to see if there is anything Father Alder needs me to do, but don't expect any more than that. And by the way, don't think I'm doing this for them." Lisi heard the disdain in his voice when he said 'them.' "I'm doing it for Father Alder."

"If you turn your back on these poor shells of human beings you are turning your back on God." Mrs. Hertz lowered her voice to a whisper.

"God has already turned His back on me. What does it matter, then, if I turn my back on Him?"

"Otto, how can you say that?"

"How can YOU ask me that? Look around you, Anika. Where are your three boys? Are they alive? Are they dead? They're under the command of a monster while he rules our entire country. And what about our friends? Where are the Wassermanns? The Tabels? Where are the Feldmans, Anika? Huh? Tell me, are they safe? My carpentry work suffers because there are no Jews to pay me for my services, and how much longer will the Nazis use me? It is a good thing I am so good at what I do. But where is God, Anika, that He would allow all this? No, I am finished with Him."

The Wassermanns. Lisi pictured the times when she and Sara would spend hours swimming in the community pool. No war, no Nazis. Just her, and Sara, and Rose.

Lisi squeezed her eyes shut as she willed the memory to go away. But it didn't. Opening her eyes, she asked the same question her papa just asked. *Where was God? Where was He that night, and where was He now? And Sara. Was she still alive at Fritz's camp?*

She never heard any answers. Now, she listened from the living room as her papa scraped his chair against the kitchen floor. She saw him grab his coat and hat and slam the front door. The eerie quiet that lingered sent shivers down Lisi's spine. She took a deep breath and padded into the kitchen, where her mama sat at the table staring into her cup. Without a word Lisi went to her and for once she comforted her mama in her arms, instead of the other way around.

Within seconds the front door opened. "What did he forget now?"

Lisi shrugged, not sure what to say. A sound in the doorway startled them both as a woman dressed in rags burst into the kitchen surrounded by a disgusting stench. She looked crazy, jittery, as she searched the room, grabbing any food she could find. Mrs. Hertz jumped from her chair, knocking it over. Before she could do anything more, Mr. Hertz took the woman by the shoulders and, as gently as he could, led her toward the door. He turned his head back and looked at his wife. "See? Imagine if I hadn't come back." Then he left with the woman.

"I think I'll stay home. They have enough help at the church today." Lisi rested her head against her mama's shoulders, feeling the need to support her.

CHAPTER 8

Lisi never paid much attention to the ugly, stinky pile of manure that graced her view from the kitchen window until one night when she couldn't bear to listen to another minute of her papa's yelling. Even though she wasn't permitted outside after dark, Lisi didn't think anyone would miss her. She quietly closed the door and snuck out to do some thinking. Her papa said a lot of mean things. She didn't know where to go. She stumbled on a little dip in the land behind the manure pile and cried. Completely hidden from not only the road but also from her own house, she decided to stay there until her tears dried up.

The stars glowed brightly that night over the fields, stretching as far as the eye could see. She thought about Sara and her family and the others whose lives had been turned upside down. She remembered asking her family what a Jew was, but she received only short replies.

One of her sisters told her Sara Wassermann was Jewish and that was why she couldn't swim with Lisi in the community pool anymore. That was the year Lisi learned, even though all people have two eyes, two ears, a nose and a mouth, it wasn't enough to protect them. From that night on, Lisi often hid behind the pile when she needed to be alone or just to think.

Over six years later Lisi still sought solace there. Unfortunately, with the Berger's basement now serving as the nearest air raid shelter, Lisi couldn't always count on complete isolation when she needed it. A lock now secured the door of the shed too. Lisi wasn't positive, but she assumed it had something to do with her brothers' Resistance meetings. Many nights Lisi and her parents would be woken from a deep sleep by a loud, blaring siren warning of impending danger. With the threat of a bomb possibly exploding in the air above, her family would quickly jump out of their beds and stumble behind the pile, around the back of the barn, to the basement stairs.

For some reason, on those nights Lisi felt safer knowing the pile sat there to block them from the road even though the air raids identified the threat of planes overhead. Tonight, she found herself again down in the depths of the shelter on a featherbed that rested atop a stiff wooden board carelessly laid between potato sacks. The latest argument between her parents weighed on her heavily and she was glad for the air raid distraction.

Her papa hadn't come home last night after the fight. Lisi didn't care. She hoped maybe a Nazi soldier took him for a spy and imprisoned him forever. No such luck. She had been sitting with her mama at the kitchen table talking when he stormed in. He was in a terrible mood. Worse than ever. He tried to hide it, but Lisi noticed bruises on the back of his neck and dried blood caked on his hands. She thought he limped too, but she couldn't be sure. Usually her mama noticed everything, but she had been so preoccupied with the refugees she barely looked at her husband.

Lisi was thankful for school tomorrow even though as long as she stayed out of her papa's way most days he left her alone. Tonight, he positioned himself on the opposite side of the tiny shelter. Her mama sat by him. *Why did she still care?*

The sounds of unfamiliar voices drifted down from the top of the stairs. Lisi looked up to see three pairs of old, worn shoes quickly descending the staircase. The last pair belonged to a woman who awkwardly carried a young child. As the family reached the bottom, Lisi cringed. It was Ruth, the refugee girl from the church. *Why were they here? Why weren't they in Father Alder's shelter?* Lisi had to admit she was a little curious about the girl but not enough to fight her brother just to talk to her.

Rose and her family followed and finally Mr. and Mrs. Berger. A few other families had already settled in.

Mrs. Hertz gave up her makeshift seat for Ruth's mama and her little brother, who accepted it gratefully. Lisi stared as her papa's face changed from his usual anger to pleasantness as he introduced himself to her and started a conversation. She hadn't seen him smile like that in a long time. From the expression on her mama's face it hadn't gone unnoticed to her, either. Lisi's stomach felt so tight she thought she would be sick.

"Lisi?" Rose stared at her. "It's my turn to guess. Are you ready?" Lisi and Rose had a word game going from the last air raid. It was Lisi's turn to come up with word for Rose.

She knew it wasn't a nice thing to do, but she couldn't help it. In honor of her papa, the next word she chose was Verräter, or traitor. Rose guessed almost every word she could think of. Lisi missed her final guess as she caught Ruth staring at her over Rose's shoulder. "Um, what?" Laughing at Rose, she knew her cover was blown.

"What are you looking at, Lisi? Come on, tell me your word." Rose looked over her shoulder and then at Lisi.

"It's nothing," she replied, but it wasn't nothing because Lisi felt like a prisoner in the interrogation room from the stares Ruth sent her way. Why did she feel like she should invite her to play? She didn't want to. Lisi wanted Rose all to herself and didn't want to share. But the girl looked so sad, and Lisi remembered the bruises on her arms and the pity she felt for her. Then she remembered Ruth's brother. Right now he was occupied, but what if he tried to hurt her if she talked to Ruth?

"Lisi? Lisi? What is wrong with you?"

Lisi stared at Ruth, then Rose, and felt something deep inside, almost as if someone was telling her what to do. She wondered if it was God. "Rose, let's ask Ruth to play with us."

"Who's Ruth?" Rose looked utterly confused, as if she didn't even know they were there.

"See that girl over there behind you in the corner? That's Ruth. She's a refugee. I saw her the other day. She looks lonely."

"I saw her family when we arrived here. My mama told me Father Alder's shelter is filled and they need to disperse the refugees between the remaining shelters. I'd rather stay home and take my chances with the bombs than share a shelter, but my mama warned me about saying anything."

Lisi stared, horrified at her friend. "What did you just say?"

"I said, I don't want to talk to her. She looks like an enemy. I don't want to play with her. You can go, just don't bring her back here."

Rose's voice escalated at the end, and Lisi wondered if Ruth heard. She felt so confused and hurt. Rose was her best friend, her only best friend since Sara left, and now she wanted to do the right thing. She never thought her best friend would turn her back, to mark Ruth as the enemy. How could a girl just like them be considered the enemy?

Bombers interrupted her thought as they flew overhead somewhere nearby. Rose grabbed Lisi's arm. The room filled with commotion as the ground above shook, dropping dirt particles on their heads. "That was the closest they've ever been." Mr. Hertz spoke obnoxiously loudly.

"Don't worry, we're safe in here."

Rose leaned over and whispered in Lisi's ear. "Mr. Berger thinks he knows everything, but I think he's just a pompous jerk. Watch his eyebrows when he talks. They look like two caterpillars dancing." Rose giggled but quickly stopped when she caught her mama's stare.

"Herr Berger has always been nice to me." Lisi shrugged her shoulder, but then again she had never really noticed his eyebrows. She looked up to see her mama staring at her from across the tiny room. What was the big deal? Why did they have to be quiet — so they could listen to the planes flying and bombs dropping, taking bets to see if they landed on them?

The sound of crying carried across the room and Lisi looked over to see Ruth wrap her arms around her little brother. Lisi's mama always taught her to do the right thing. Befriending Ruth was the right thing to do, Lisi knew. She watched her mama, Mrs. Berger, and Mrs. Meyer approach Ruth's mama. Lisi closed her eyes wishing she could sink into the floor. She knew what her mama was doing. Through squinted eyes she peered out as her mama beckoned another neighbor, Mrs. Weber, to join them. The three women always prayed together during the air raids but this time Mrs. Hertz invited Mrs. Weber to pray with them for Ruth's family. Lisi hoped that with the addition of Ruth's family her mama would refrain from the possibility of embarrassment, especially because Mrs. Weber had no alms about expressing her disdain for the refugees in town.

Her hopes quickly dissipated as Mrs. Weber crossed the small room and squeezed herself in between Mrs. Berger and Mrs. Meyer, forcing Mrs. Meyer closer to Ruth's mama. The whistle of another bomb screeched through the air and Lisi found herself taking solace in the prayers of her mama.

When the prayers finished Lisi discreetly motioned her hands absentmindedly in the sign of the cross as she thought about Rose's previous comment about Ruth. Then she thought how brave her mama was to pray with a stranger, regardless of her religion. *Go talk to the poor girl, Lisi.* Where did that come from? *Yes, I should go talk to her,* her thoughts replied. For some reason, though, Rose's words and the fear of her best friend's rejection won. As she sat there, staring at the stranger only feet away, more threads in the tapestry of her make-believe world unraveled, creating a brand new tear. This one, she feared, could ruin a great friendship.

CHAPTER 9

Needing to think, Lisi wrapped her sweater tighter around her as she sat behind the manure pile on a blanket under the stars. Today Ruth and her brother Peter had come to school for the first time. It was two days after the night of the air raid. They'd only been in town one week and now the refugees invaded her school too. How awful of her to think that. Was she letting Rose's influence rub off on her? Shortly after Ruth's brother began to cry the sound of the planes grew faint and Lisi and her family were able to return to their beds.

She looked around her and laughed at the irony of her situation. Behind a pile of animal manure was the only place she felt safe now. In some ways she felt like that pile. At first it seemed to be a pile of waste, despised, rejected, and unwanted. But after time as it matured, it's purpose clearer, it became like a priceless gem. She started to sing a silly song about it. "Here I am, despised like this manure, they say it turns to gold, how can I be sure?" She was no priceless gem yet, for sure. Lisi felt more like the unwanted waste as she thought about how she purposefully avoided

Ruth's eyes the other night and pushed her way up the shelter stairs so she could run home before Ruth's family even reached the bottom step.

Her thoughts drifted to Fritz and Albert as she looked at the shed. Fritz still walked with a limp, barely on the way to recovery before being drafted back into the prison he had just escaped from. "God," she whispered into the still, quiet night. "Are you listening? If so, please take care of all my brothers. Please protect them and bring them home safely." She closed her eyes and felt a breeze on her face. A shiver ran over her, but she had a feeling it wasn't from the cold winter air.

Maybe God was listening after all. She smiled and lifted her chin to let the strange but thrilling sensation wash over her. She thought about how God had answered so many prayers. After all, Fritz came home to them once already. Lisi thought about that wonderful day last summer. He walked with a bad limp, and looked like death had already claimed him, but he was home.

Lisi and Rose had been picking potatoes out in the Meyer's field. That day had felt like a hundred degrees, too hot for their normal race to see who could fill their sack first. Instead they talked about Ludwig, a boy from the other side of town. The conversation ended abruptly when a very wounded soldier on crutches hobbled down the road, stopping at the edge of the yard. It had been four years since Lisi had seen Fritz last, but she recognized the body posture immediately. After a quick explanation to Rose, Lisi forgot all about her potato picking and ran to welcome her stepbrother home. That night was a joyous night for Mrs. Hertz and Lisi, but a bittersweet time for Fritz, who struggled with the realization of how much the war stole from him. His first night home Lisi overheard him talk to their mama after her papa left the house. Fritz had celebrated his thirtieth birthday in the spring. If the war hadn't come, he probably would have been married by now with his own place far away from his stepfather.

Lisi shivered and pulled the blanket up around her. Yes, that was a good night for her and her mama. She shifted her body to position herself facing away from her house and stared at the small shed. "God, I want to do something to make a difference. I want to be of some use in this war but I don't know how. Is this the answer?" Lisi felt more confused than ever. Was she really only supposed to feed the refugees? Was that enough? She didn't know them. There had to be more. When she and Ruth made eye contact at school, she thought about saying hello but instead only smiled weakly. Like Rose said, they were visitors, passing through, and she'd lost enough friends. Why would she want to get attached just to be hurt again? She didn't know then that the thing she feared the most would become the one thing to keep her going.

CHAPTER 10

The refugee invasion, as Rose coined it, had occurred three weeks ago. Many families still remained, and it didn't seem like they were in a hurry to leave. Ruth and her family stayed at the church, but with the number of refugees arriving daily, more doors of vacant houses opened to the visitors. At school Lisi managed to distract herself. Saturdays, however, were different. Her mama expected her to accompany her to the church to help. During school was one thing, but what if Father Alder assigned her to Ruth's section? He handed out assignments like an officer to his soldiers.

Last Saturday Lisi faked an illness. Her mama saw through her. Fortunately, that day Father Alder assigned her far away from Ruth and Rose. Oh, she still loved her best friend, but things had changed. To anyone who didn't know the girls intimately it appeared as if nothing could come between them.

Lisi hadn't realized the strain that tugged on their friendship until one morning, a few days ago, when her mama offered to have Rose for dinner that night. It had been just the two of them home for a week this time, and the house felt more empty than usual. "Little One?" Her mama asked as Lisi hesitated.

"Uh, sure, Mama. I'll talk to her today." Lisi wouldn't talk to Rose. Not about coming over for dinner, anyway.

"Is there something going on between you two?"

Good question. They walked to school together as usual and ate lunch together, but something definitely seemed different. "I'm not sure exactly." Lisi felt uncomfortable when Rose talked about the refugees as if they were something awful. Thoughtfully, she added, "It just doesn't feel the same, Mama. Rose's family helps the refugees just like we do, but it's different. She's different." Her eyes begged for help.

"You know, it's a little tight anyway right now, I'm not even sure we have enough food. Let's plan for a nice cozy meal together just you and me next to the warm heater tonight."

Lisi knew her mama would give anyone the food off her own plate, and she was grateful her mama understood. She felt torn. She wanted to please Rose but deep inside she longed to talk to Ruth also. That voice inside her grew with each day that passed, and Lisi had to try hard to ignore it. This morning when she woke she couldn't pretend anymore that it would disappear. She made a decision to go to the church with her mama and talk to Ruth.

"Little One, what's bothering you?" Lisi felt her mama's arm wrap around her shoulders, but it offered little comfort. She bit her lip and took a deep breath. Even though she always felt better after a good conversation with her mama, how could she talk to her about this?

"Mama?" She hesitated, not knowing how to complete her question without disappointing her mama.

"Mmm?"

"Have you ever had a feeling deep inside that you needed to do something, the right thing, but you were too afraid to do it?" There. She'd said it. Her faults exposed themselves, lying out in the open for everyone to see. Lisi looked to the ground, waiting.

Her mama stopped walking and lifted Lisi's chin until their eyes met. In a gentle voice, she replied, "Of course, I have. Do you remember the day Mr. Richter paid us a visit not long after the war began?" Lisi nodded. How could she forget? The one defining moment when she knew she wanted the same faith her mama had. According to her, luck was something people believed in when they had nothing else. Her mama always said how fortunate they were to have a God that they could believe in and rely on, so there was never need for luck.

That day Lisi had just walked in the door from school, ready to rid her mind of mathematics and literature. Closing the door behind her, she yelled toward the kitchen her usual hello to her mama. Only silence greeted her.

Curious, Lisi walked toward the kitchen. Mama was always preparing dinner at this time or cleaning up. "Mama?" Silence.

An eerie feeling coursed through Lisi's body alerting her senses. The hairs on her arms rose and her head pricked at the sensation. Quietly, she slipped off her shoes and crept toward the kitchen doorway. As a last minute thought she grabbed her papa's umbrella, fully aware that it offered no better protection than a potato sack.

She took two steps and heard a familiar voice that made her heart beat twice as fast. "Hello, Lisi. How was school today?"

Mr. Richter? Lisi approached the doorway to find her mama standing near the table, gripping the back of a chair, while Mr. Richter stood just inside the kitchen. His large frame seemed to take up the entire room, not to mention his intimidating manner. He wore a jacket even though it was summer, and he held something in his hand that looked like a pad of paper.

Blocking her path to her mama, Mr. Richter repeated his question with a calm, smooth voice that made even the hairs on her legs rise.

"Lisi, answer Mr. Richter, please." Mrs. Hertz's voice didn't match her body expressions, but Lisi obeyed.

"Good afternoon, Mr. Richter. School was fine, thank you for asking." Lisi forced herself to steady her voice so he couldn't hear the fear, although she thought he must be able to smell it — couldn't dogs smell fear?

"Mr. Richter, as I was saying, I'm sorry but Otto is at work. Can I help you with something?" The words came out shaky and quiet.

Even before Mr. Richter took over Mr. Wassermann's office, Lisi had been afraid of him. His personality fit the perfect Nazi image. His son, Gunther, grew up with Fritz and now he kept the "peace" around town, which meant he could strut up and down the streets in uniform like a bullying peacock without any trouble. Freddie was younger but the nicest of them all.

"I'm not here for small talk, Anika. It's time you and Otto joined us." Mr. Richter stepped toward her, opening a gap for Lisi to sneak behind him into the kitchen. He shoved the pad toward Mrs. Hertz. Reaching into his pocket, he pulled out a pen and thrust it in her face.

"I...I don't understand what you're talking about. But anything that needs to be signed, I really must talk to Otto."

"You will sign this, or else." He shoved a gun under her mama's chin. Lisi never saw the writing on the pad, but it wasn't difficult for her to know that he wanted her parents to sign a confirmation of their allegiance to the Nazi movement.

Somehow Someone was watching over them because, as Lisi held her breath, she watched her mama gracefully slip away from the gun and slowly walk into the living room. Mr. Richter followed her every move. Mrs. Hertz walked back to face him, clutching her well-worn Bible.

Lisi witnessed a transformation in her mama right before her eyes. It seemed almost otherworldly. Standing tall, Mrs. Hertz raised the Bible over her head and proclaimed in a strong, firm voice, "This is the party I belong to." Without moving, she matched Mr. Richter's glare. After what seemed to Lisi like a lifetime, he slid the gun back into his coat pocket, turned, and left the house slamming the door behind him.

Lisi slowly released her breath. Only after her mama exhaled did she run to her. "Oh, Mama, you were wonderful! How did you do that?" She threw her arms around her mama's waist.

"It was all God, Little One, only God. If we trust in Him, He will deliver us from evil." Lisi remembered those words her mama had said just before she left the room to finish dinner.

Lisi was young, but even then she knew how much she wanted to be strong like that. To be brave and courageous. Where was that bravery now?

"Mama, you said you were afraid to do the right thing, but you did it. How? I'm afraid, but instead of doing it I've been running from it because of my fears. I don't feel brave at all, and I'm scared of ruining my friendship with Rose."

She slowed down, sensing how much of a disappointment she was to her mama. The faith her mama had didn't exist in her at all. Maybe she was never meant to be brave.

"First of all, my Little One, you are very brave." Mrs. Hertz stopped and picked Lisi's chin up. "Look at what you're doing here each weekend with Rose and the others. It takes a lot of courage to spend your days helping them and taking the time to talk to them."

"Second, I was terrified from one end of my body to the other. Part of me wanted to give in because it would be easier." This wasn't the first time Lisi wondered what life might have been like if her parents supported Hitler. She also wondered how it might have changed her brothers.

"But I knew if I gave in I would have become the biggest coward. God helps us through anything. The more we pray and read the Bible, the more we can hear

His voice when we need it. That day, He told me to be brave and encouraged me to remember who the real God was. Then I found a strength that seemed to come from somewhere else. But don't be deceived. I was very much afraid, and it took everything in me not to run away from doing the right thing.

Lisi felt her mama's eyes on her but kept silent, afraid her voice would crack from the emotion in her throat. Her mama grabbed her hand, and Lisi felt her love and bravery even through the mittens.

"And finally," Mrs. Hertz continued, "your friendship with Rose runs deeper and stronger than all this nonsense going on around here. She is your best friend, so she'll come around. You'll see." Her mama sounded confident, but Lisi knew deep down she only said it for Lisi's benefit. War did funny things to people. Neighbor turned against neighbor, friend against friend, and even family member against each other.

A new sense of boldness flowed through her veins. When it reached the top of her body she stood a little taller and lifted her head. She *could* do this. She prayed a short prayer asking God to help her grow bold like He helped her mama. Sooner than later they arrived at the steps of St. Kilian, and she wondered if she could really be brave. She'd find out soon.

CHAPTER 11

Vacant homes stood all around town, yet the church basement still housed the majority of the refugees. It had been organized in rows from one end to the other, blankets and bedding laid out from corner to corner, some with multiple people to one bed. They looked just like Lisi imagined the people who died at Fritz's work camp. Shadows of life, despair colored faces that once held hope. The only space to walk in the room were two rows that divided beds. These rows allowed people to have a place to walk and distribute food. Lisi knew Father Alder also had people living in the empty rooms in his home. Rumor had it that they were mostly younger, single women, but Lisi hadn't ever been in his house nor did she have any desire to.

As they walked through the door, Lisi didn't need to search for Ruth. She knew her bed in the middle row, center of the room, which was a good thing for them because it was warmer. Lisi knew many of the refugees slept in the extra hats and coats donated by families in town.

She scanned the room and noticed the newcomers. Then she found Ruth, lost in a book borrowed from someone in town. She looked so content, Lisi didn't want to interrupt her. Was she alone? Lisi looked around for Peter and saw him with a boy and their mama and brother talking with another family. Excitement grew in her stomach. She uttered a small thank you to God for this time alone, and she knew she couldn't wait any longer.

With determined steps, Lisi put a smile on her face and marched over. Ruth looked up. "Hi. It's Ruth, isn't it?"

Ruth narrowed her eyes and tugged on her right ear. Lisi realized she had caught her off guard. And why shouldn't she have been? Lisi had given her the cold shoulder more than once at school and practically ignored her during the air raid. She was tempted to give up, say she tried, and walk away from the whole thing, but something inside her wouldn't let her.

Bending down, she extended her hand to the familiar stranger. "I'm Lisi."

Ruth hugged herself and looked down. Lisi wondered what was so interesting about her lap but chose not to ask. Maybe Ruth didn't understand what she said, but she doubted that. She tried again. After all, she had come this far. Might as well go all the way.

She patted her chest. Maybe Ruth was a Soviet. "I'm Lisi." She waited. Nothing. No response, not even a glance. Fine. If Ruth wanted to be that way, that was her problem. Lisi stood and huffed. She did her part. She reached out only to be rejected. As Lisi turned to find her mama, she noticed a tear trickle down Ruth's cheek. When she looked to where Peter stood, he was staring at her.

What was their problem? Who cared? She wouldn't be bothered with them anymore.

That night, lying in bed, Lisi couldn't stop thinking about Ruth. At first, she was offended that the girl didn't accept her attempt to be friends. The more she thought about it, however, the more Lisi knew there was something else. She knew what the war had done and still did to her own family, yet couldn't imagine what it had done to Ruth's.

Her parents starting arguing in their bedroom. Lisi rolled her eyes and plopped the pillow across her face. Yes, things had changed. Her family was not only separated but divided. Lisi wondered how much more Ruth had gone through, that she had to leave her home and go to a strange place, and without her papa.

Two days later Ruth wasn't at school. Lisi played with the idea of asking Peter about it, but then she remembered the way he had looked at her. She watched the way he talked to a few of the other boys. He laughed and there was something very attractive about him. Maybe it was the dimple in his left cheek or the blonde piece of wave that tumbled down his forehead. Either way, to Lisi's astonishment, she wanted to get to know him.

She also had a feeling inside this was what God wanted her to do. After school that day she asked her mama if they could go to the church. She never told her exactly what happened the other day, so she quickly filled her in. "You can go on your own. I'll stay here and prepare dinner." Lisi kissed her mama and with a renewed bounce in her step, headed for the church.

As she entered the room, Lisi spotted her papa on the other side. He stood, talking and laughing with a woman she didn't know. She had forgotten he came here to help Father Alder sometimes. She was curious who it was but didn't let herself lose her focus of this mission.

Ruth sat in the same position. The only difference was the book in her hand. Lisi didn't recognize it. She also noticed Ruth sat alone again, and she was thankful for that. She didn't know how she would be able to talk to her with Peter stalking them.

She took a deep breath and put on a full smile. Then she lifted her head and strode down the aisle. Lisi knew she looked more confident than she felt. Too soon she arrived in front of Ruth.

"Hi, Ruth, I'm Lisi." She held her breath as she extended her hand. This time Ruth looked at her. Progress.

"I know." The words struck Lisi and her head jerked, but she relaxed when Ruth took her hand and shook it. A moment of awkwardness passed between the girls before Ruth spoke again. "Would you like to sit down?"

Lisi noticed how she quickly hid the book under her blankets. "I'd love to." Now what? What did you say to someone who had probably experienced horrors in the past few months that you couldn't even imagine? Lisi tried to think of something to say, but her mind blanked. "Uh, how's your leg?"

Ruth looked at her, confused. "I'm not sure what you mean."

"The day you came to our town, I saw you. You walked with crutches. Was it your foot?"

"Oh, that." Ruth laughed.

"I'm glad you find my concern for your health humorous." How dare she laugh at her. Lisi almost walked away.

Ruth stopped. "I'm so sorry. I wasn't laughing at you. I didn't remember I had them. They weren't real. They were to make the Soviets think I was crippled. Then they would leave me alone." She changed the subject before Lisi could ask more. "How old are you?"

"Twelve. How about you?"

"Thirteen." She pointed with her thumb to where her brother stood. "My brother, Peter, is also thirteen. We're twins. My little brother, Henry, is four. He's over there with Mama."

Lisi knew what Henry looked like, but she pretended to look again. In truth she didn't want to look at him. She couldn't imagine what he must have gone through in his short life. "I have a brother named Henry, too. Actually, I have three brothers and two sisters. Well, one brother is really my stepbrother, but he's like my real brother. I'm the youngest. My two sisters live in Wurzburg. All three of my brothers are fighting in the war, but they don't like Hitler. At least two of them don't — I don't think. I'm not sure about my brother Henry. He volunteered when he was only fifteen. He's twenty-one now. My papa was so furious he hollered loudly enough that I thought the ceiling would collapse right on us."

What was the matter with her? Lisi always seemed to talk more when she felt nervous. She certainly didn't need to give an entire account of her family history to this stranger, no matter how much she wanted to help her. So why did she feel compelled to add that part about her papa? Was she embarrassed about Henry? Surely Ruth didn't think anything. Lisi made sure not to mention that her papa wasn't fighting, since Ruth's papa must be in the war and that explained his absence.

"Is your papa fighting in the war?" Why not ask what she was thinking? Immediately she regretted her impulsive question when tears glistened at the corners of Ruth's eyes and her arms instinctively wrapped around her middle. "I'm sorry," she stammered. "I just thought, since he wasn't with you."

She let the sentence drop. Ruth began to cry, and Lisi noticed Peter look their way. *Great,* she thought, *he's coming over and I made his sister cry.* Lisi felt like a cornered mouse. Should she run away or cower in the corner, waiting to be eaten?

She decided it would be safer to run, but then who knew what she would run into. She gently put her hand on her arm. "Ruth, I'm so sorry. Please forgive me."

She didn't know what to do. Peter was just feet away when Ruth reached out and wrapped her arms around Lisi's neck. Lisi startled but relaxed when she felt Ruth's body shake from her sobs. Peter froze in place. She watched his face transform, from startled to confused to angry. She turned her head away and somewhat shyly put her arms gently around Ruth's back and let her cry. Who cared what Peter said? Something made itself right, inside of her, and it made her feel good. She felt needed. Important. And brave! Maybe her mama was right. Maybe this was what being brave was all about. Maybe this was her role in the war. She hoped so, because she hadn't felt this good in a long time.

CHAPTER 12

After a few minutes Ruth sat back and wiped her eyes. "I'm so sorry. That was rude of me." She looked at Lisi then noticed Peter. "Oh, Peter, this is Lisi. She's my new friend."

New friend. Lisi liked that. She held on to the bravery long enough to rise and extend her hand to Peter, though she hardly expected him to accept it. To her surprise he reached out and shook it, though the expression on his face told her he didn't trust her one bit. She didn't care. She didn't need his trust. She only wanted Ruth's.

The unexpected feeling that shot like a lightning bolt from her hand to her stomach when Peter's hand touched hers was unexpected. She pulled away quickly just in case it flowed through her into him. Taking a step backward she stammered, "It's nice to meet you."

Did Peter feel it too? If he did he covered it a lot better than she did. He gave her a short nod and checked his sister over with his eyes. Satisfied, he left and rejoined his friend.

"Please forgive my brother, Lisi. He's a little protective. We've gone through a lot, and he is having a hard time handling it. You see, my papa started out this trip with us. He was old when this war began and had been injured in the Great War, making it difficult for him to walk. Much of my family started with us. We were only two days in when the Red Army reached us on one side and the Nazi Army surprised us from the other side. We had stopped to rest for Papa and a few others who needed it. Many of the men in our group had been prepared to fight if we were attacked." Ruth stopped, and Lisi waited.

"We all scattered as soldiers and civilians fought everywhere. Mama took Henry and ran to a thicket of trees in one direction, but I was blocked by the fighting, so I ran the opposite way. Peter stayed to help Papa and my grossvater and the other men." Lisi knew what happened before Ruth continued. Two men, one boy, only one boy survived. Lisi wanted to cry for Ruth but also for herself as she thought of her brothers.

"I watched from the trees as Papa and Opa died right in front of me. Peter was hurt and fell, but he managed to survive by pretending he was dead. My poor brother spent hours face down in mud. As I watched my papa fall to the ground, I felt someone grab my arms from behind like this." Lisi watched as Ruth demonstrated. That explained the bruises. "I knew he was an Ivan by the way he spoke. Before I knew what happened, he threw me to the ground. I screamed for help, but my scream became lost in the chorus of screams all around. He hit the back of my head so hard into the ground it knocked me unconscious. When

I woke, I found myself lying in a field and my body hurt all over.

"Peter was right there waiting for me to wake up. I didn't realize how bad I looked." Lisi knew why Peter cried for his sister. "He found Mama and Henry and carried me with the group out of the way of combat. About half of our group died in the woods that day. I will never get back what was lost. Neither will all the other women and girls. And for what? Such a waste! I wish they were all dead!"

Lisi understood exactly how Ruth felt. Why were her brothers fighting? Was it really worth all the bloodshed and hatred and division it caused? And the brutality Ruth and her family received for no reason other than for sport. Lisi hurt for Ruth. She leaned over and gave her new friend a hug. "I am so sorry for what happened to you, Ruth. I don't know what else to say. It's terrible. I want to help you."

CHAPTER 13

"**I** am so proud of you, Little One. You are blossoming into a backfisch, quite a young lady, not a little girl anymore. You stepped out in fear to do what you knew was right. God will honor that for sure." The way her mama made her feel so loved, Lisi doubted that she'd need anything from her papa. They sat together in the living room as Lisi shared her encounter with Ruth. Her papa stayed at the church long after she left, trying to find homes for some of the refugee families. How ironic, he was so willing to help Father Alder find temporary homes but he wouldn't let anyone come to stay in theirs. He was a hypocrite, and Lisi liked him even less for that.

Lisi smiled at her mama's compliment then frowned. "But it took me a long time to do it."

"Lisi, listen to me." Her mama's voice was stern, but gentle. "We all have decisions to make each day. Some are easy and some are more difficult. Some are easy in our hearts, yet difficult for us to carry out. If you continue to read this and don't ever stop praying, those difficult decisions become possible." Lisi looked at the worn Bible her mama held up and wondered if she wasn't just talking about Lisi's decision to help Ruth and the refugees today. Could it be possible that her mama knew about Fritz and Albert?

"Mama?" Her mama seemed far away. "Mama. You're not talking about me, are you?"

Mrs. Hertz stared at her, and Lisi saw the struggle in her eyes. She knew for sure now. This was the moment when her mama would either tell her everything or lie to hide her secrets. Lisi's stomach rolled. Part of her wanted to know everything, but she remembered what Fritz told her not so very long ago about knowing too much.

"No, I'm not. I knew something quite a few years ago, but I let fear keep me from doing something about it. And because of it, people were hurt. I promised myself and God I would never let that happen again." Lisi waited for more, but her mama carefully chose her words. Curiosity overruled her common sense.

"Tell me." She may regret it, but if her mama felt the same way she did and didn't do something because she was afraid, Lisi needed to know.

"What I am about to tell you is not to leave this room. Understand?" Lisi nodded. "It was the night of Kristallnacht." Lisi's jaw began to tremble. Why does this night keep coming back to haunt her? "I knew beforehand that something was going to happen that night."

Lisi ran her hands over her hair and pushed up her sleeves. The temperature in the room suddenly seemed to rise twenty degrees. "I don't understand."

Her mama answered with one word. "Henry."

"Henry? Tell me, Mama. Please?"

"Henry came home from school that afternoon looking deeply troubled. When I asked him about it, he tried to hide it from me. Of course, he couldn't. I found him alone in his room on the bed with his head in his hands. Then he told me. He had overheard Gunther Richter and Hans Schmidt formulating a plan." From the time they were young, Hans was always a little different. He never thought about the consequences until it was too late, just like his older brother, Derrik.

Mrs. Hertz briefly explained to Lisi a little of what took place between Henry and Gunther. The boys grew closer when they both joined the Hitler Youth Program at the same time. They would often have quiet conversations together, agreeing that Hitler and his ideals were punch-drunk, or crazy. Something happened and Gunther changed.

There were no more side conversations, no more glazed looks in Gunther's eyes during classes. Slowly there evolved something more. Something that started to concern Henry but gradually grew into fear. Gunther had been brainwashed. By his parents. By the Reich. He began to believe the lies Hitler spewed out. Ideas like, 'There must be no tenderness in youth. I want to see in their eyes the gleam of the beast of prey.' He really believed that he belonged to a supreme race, and therefore his job was to rid the world of the inferiors. He clung to Hitler's promise, 'Today, Germany; tomorrow, the world.'

"That night, Henry knew immediately what was happening at the Wassermann's. Their head teacher had been interrupted at the start of class by one of his leaders, and Henry used that moment to exit the room to use the restroom. He overheard the words "Munich", "retribution", and "Ernst vom Rath". After class, the two boys met in the corner. They were engaged in intense conversation. He said they showed a passion of fury in their eyes."

Mrs. Hertz took a deep breath. "In order to prevent anything from happening here, Henry snuck out later that night in an attempt to divert the incidents." She told how he had crept down the road in the shadows at 22:00, unsure of the exact meeting time or location. He made his way through the entire town in record time. He began at the outskirts where Hans lived and snaked through the streets to Gunther's house. His primary goal was to intercept them before they began. He had it all planned out, what he was going to say, something about relaying an important message he overheard from one of their leaders about a change in plans.

"Unfortunately, Henry lagged just seconds behind them for an entire hour. He finally located them when he crossed the street around 23:00. That's when he heard the screams here.

"When he arrived, he was too horrified to think clearly as he watched the attack on the Wassermanns. My poor boy! He told me he just stood, dumbfounded. Finally, Gunther led Hans down the road to the next victims on their list."

Lisi couldn't breathe. Her mama continued through small sobs. "I knew, and I didn't do anything to help them.

My young son was braver than me. He even endured an interrogation from your Papa."

Lisi remembered that day. "Henry, where were you last night during all this?" Henry turned his gaze to meet his father's unwavering stare and absently touched his ribs.

"His ribs should have hurt him because of a fight with the boys, he told me."

Lisi answered with realization. "But he didn't try to stop them, so that's not why."

"No, that wasn't why. He told me he helped Mr. Wassermann into his house, and as he did he tripped on the stairs, landing on his ribs."

Lisi remembered the second time her papa asked Henry where he had been. He hadn't answered him yet, and her papa grew angrier and angrier. But before he answered, Henry caught Lisi looking at him with questions in her eyes. She remembered he returned her questions with a pleading look and a slight shake of his head, then met their papa square in the face. "I went out to try to stop it. I knew they were planning something. I overheard them."

"Really. That's all you had to go on? What's the matter with you, boy? Did you hear any reliable sources discuss this?" Henry could clearly see by the hard stare and the criticism in his voice that his father didn't believe a word he said.

"Otto, let him be." Henry closed his eyes and wished his mother would stop protecting him.

"That's the problem, Anika! You baby him. You baby all of them. Maybe if you let him become a man, he'd start acting like one. 'A youth will grow up before which the world will shrink back.'" Lisi remembered those words even now. Hitler had said them, and that was the first time her papa quoted anything from Hitler. Lisi had felt Henry's gaze as she sat stone still in her chair while a tear trickled down her face. He knew she was thinking about her best friend.

Lisi stared at her mama in disbelief as she finished the story. She remembered the entire conversation, the look on Henry's face. "Lisi, I am so sorry. It's my fault the Wassermanns and Baehrs and everyone else suffered through that. I could have helped them escape beforehand, but I was a coward."

She could tell her mama wanted to tell her more, but something stopped her. Lisi desperately wanted to ask if she was helping Fritz and Henry in the Resistance, but she couldn't. What if her mama didn't know? Then Fritz would never trust her again and she could put them in danger. But, oh, if she could only talk to her mama about it. Mrs. Hertz stood up to get ready for bed. The conversation was over.

CHAPTER 14

"He thinks you're a snob."

Lisi shot Ruth a sideways glance as she kept most of her focus on Peter, a little ahead of them. Ever since she stepped out of her comfort zone that day and befriended Ruth, the girls became instant friends. The church was on Lisi's way home from school so every day after school the girls walked back to the church together, where they sat and talked and shared stories until Lisi needed to help her mama prepare dinner.

"What do you mean he thinks I'm a snob? He barely knows me." Lisi stopped in the middle of the road and placed her hands on her hips. Lately, a new realization was beginning to hit Lisi. She had feelings for Peter. Not the same feelings she had for Ruth or other friends. It was different. She had never felt these feelings before. Anytime she saw Peter those feelings danced around in her stomach as if they were performing on stage at the Deutsches Theater in Berlin. However, her friend's latest response to her own question may cause her to rethink that.

Ruth put her hand on Lisi's arm. "I'm sorry, Lisi. You asked me what he thought of you. I was being honest. I didn't mean to hurt your feelings. It's just that he thinks... well, he doesn't know you yet. Not really." She stopped to think. "Maybe if you, you know, sort of put your chin down a little when you talked to him, he might see you the way I see you."

Lisi's body stiffened in her own defense when she realized Ruth was right. From the beginning she had put on airs around Peter, because of the way he acted first. Of course, he was only responding to her. She realized she had been harboring hard feelings against him. If she really believed her calling in this war was to help refugees, like Ruth and her family, she had to change that. Especially since Peter was part of that family.

"You're right, Ruth. I'm sorry. I'm sure Peter is a wonderful protector and brother." Peter had already disappeared inside the church now and Lisi didn't feel ready to talk to him today. Maybe tomorrow. "Hey, wanna come to my house today?" Anything to avoid him.

Ruth agreed and slipped her arm through Lisi's. It felt good to have a new close friend, but it made Lisi sad as she thought about Rose. Over the last week the once inseparable friends rarely saw each other anymore. It started the morning Lisi was late to leave for school. The old Rose would have waited for her so they could be late together. That morning, Rose didn't seem too upset when Mrs. Hertz answered the door and relayed Lisi's message to go on without her. Since then Rose met other friends on her walk to school and Lisi now left a few minutes later.

The worst part of this was, when Lisi did see Rose, she hid like a scaredy-cat or pretended she didn't see her to avoid her. If by chance their eyes did connect, she would give a stupid looking half smile and stand there gawking until Rose returned the half smile. She wondered what Rose was doing right now.

As if planned by fate, Lisi and Ruth were passing in front of the Meyer's house, when Rose walked out. A group of Nazi soldiers approached, and Lisi watched, horrified as her friend stood tall on her step and raised her arm in response to the soldiers' salute. The speed with which Lisi pulled Ruth's arm and raced to her house almost caused both girls to stumble. Forgetting all about Peter, she shut the door but not before she caught Rose watching her from the corner of her eye.

"Are you all right?" Ruth asked.

Nodding her head, Lisi bent over her knees to catch her breath. No, she wasn't all right. They only ran a little, but she was more out of breath from what she had just witnessed. Any time she and Rose passed a soldier on the street, Rose would salute but always laughed and joked about it.

Today was different. Standing outside her door, Lisi didn't see that silliness. She saw something very different. She saw a side of Rose she had never seen before. Was it an act, or was it real? Even with all that had transpired recently, did Rose still believe in the supremacy?

"Why don't you just ask her?"

"I can't do that." The words came out more as breaths. Lisi felt sick. How could Rose not see the ugly reality behind this beautiful tapestry of lies? Surely her parents didn't believe it. She excused herself to Ruth and went to the bathroom where she could wretch in private. Had she just lost her lifelong best friend forever?

CHAPTER 15

Over the next few weeks, Mrs. Hertz managed to find a home for Ruth and her family. The girls were overjoyed when they found out it was almost directly across the street from the Hertz's. Lisi felt glad for that since Rose spent most of her time with her new friends at school, none of which included any of the refugee families. These friends saluted the Nazi soldiers with enthusiasm and dedication, friends that Lisi overheard criticize their old Jewish neighbors, and friends that speculated about certain families who did not support Hitler.

Lisi and Ruth spent hours together after school and on weekends. She had even finally managed to muster up the courage and have her first real conversation with Peter. It only took her two weeks. Once that hurdle had been jumped, Peter's protective instincts kicked into high gear and he started acting like the brother Lisi had been missing. Much to her chagrin, she realized the relationship would never go further than that of a brother and a sister. Eventually she came to accept that fact and found comfort in the brotherly love she had been missing.

As much as Lisi continued to find her calling in helping Ruth and other refugees, she slowly began to realize God saw a much bigger picture for this special friendship. The realization hit Lisi one day as the girls talked about the recent Deutsch Schützen massacre. They heard about it the night before on the Hertz family radio. The radio announcer shared that about 60 Jews had been killed at Deutsch Schützen-Eisenberg, Austria.

Lisi thought about all of her friends, especially Sara, and Ruth shared in the sorrowful ignorance of the whereabouts of several Jewish friends from home. As they talked Lisi realized that even though the two girls looked very different, Ruth was the only other friend who really saw the ugly truth behind the tapestry of lies. This realization launched the friendship to a new level for Lisi, and for that she would be grateful in the months ahead.

CHAPTER 16

March, 1945

"Lisi, the window." Lisi was already on the way to her "post" when Rille ordered the command. As much as Lisi loved having her sister home again, she didn't realize how accustomed she had become to being the only child. She and her mama were growing closer every day, and in the evening they would complete their routine as effortlessly as a singer and the orchestra working together in a flawless performance. Now, Rille was the off-key singer interrupting the beautiful music. Every time Rille bossed Lisi around she wanted to say something, but what was the point of defending herself? She knew Rille was upset about the recent bombing that hit the outskirts of Wurzburg. "Remember, Lisi, we aren't going to say anything to Rille to cause her to be more upset. Everyone responds differently to things." Her mama told her Rille was very shaken by it, but Lea decided to stay so she could keep working. Rille took the first train home, and they didn't know how long she'd stay. Lisi would do her best to be nice to her sister, especially since a big battle in the Ardennes Mountains just ended, making people believe the war would be over soon. Then Rille would be leaving anyway.

As Lisi peered out the window, her parents and Rille sat in the living room listening to the box that continued to bring them news of the world outside. Looking at her family, she thought about the fact that her papa was actually home tonight. He usually spent his evenings "helping" Father Alder when he was home.

The radio program began. Lisi strained to hear, but she couldn't disregard her responsibility at the window. Excitement entwined with apprehension filled her. What if everyone was right? What if the war really would be over soon? She was glad because she missed her brothers terribly. But at what cost? She knew her life would be different, but how? She often thought about what kind of Germany would be waiting for them at the end. Again, the Soviets invaded her thoughts. "Lord, send the Allies first."

Short prayers like these were frequent in Lisi's mind lately. She still had questions about God and her mama's faith, but she figured, what could it hurt to pray?

What was that? An orange glow lit up the sky somewhere in the distance. "Mama, Papa, I see something."

"You see something? That's all you got? What do you see?" Lisi could hear the sarcasm drip from her papa's voice.

"What is it, Little One?" Her mama rose and Lisi moved out of the way so she could see. Gasping, she cried, "Otto!"

Her papa jumped up and pushing past them, flew open the front door. The family quickly followed him, forgetting all about the radio.

"What is it?" Lisi's voice shook.

Rille stared in horror as she replied, "Wurzburg."

Inside, the radio continued to give updates on the war around the country. Then two words screamed into the room. "Bombing. Wurzburg." The sound of a vehicle shook everyone back into reality as they ran back into the house. Mrs. Hertz reached the radio first and turned it off just in time. Nobody moved or spoke as the truck drove by the house. Rille started to cry then, and Mrs. Hertz stared at the radio. Mr. Hertz didn't move.

Desperately wanting to feel comforted, Lisi struggled between bravely remaining where she stood, afraid to make any sound, or reverting back to the scared little girl. Unfortunately, the decision was made for her. Too late they all heard the sound of another army truck drive by. Would it stop in front of their house? Did it pick up on the radio signal?

Lisi released her breath as the truck continued its route. Her papa seemed ready to explode. "What is wrong with you?" He jabbed a finger at her as he continued, "you had one small job to do, and you couldn't even do that, standing there like an idiot." Tears threatened at the corners of Lisi's eyes. *I only wanted them to see what I saw. I thought I was doing something good.*

"We've all had to make sacrifices, but once again you think you're exempt. You think you're better than everyone else." He walked toward Lisi enraged. For a moment, she thought he would slap her. Instead, he passed by her to the front door where he grabbed his coat and left. Again.

CHAPTER 17

O pening her eyes Lisi immediately began to replay last night's events when the door interrupted her thoughts. Rille popped in. "Get dressed. Mama is taking you to go get Lea today."

"We're going to Wurzburg?" Lisi sat up tall, unsure if she felt more apprehension or excitement at the thought of seeing her sister.

"No, WE aren't going. You are going. I'm going to stay here and help cook at the church. Father Alder is anticipating more refugees. Hurry up. Mama will get angry."

"Is Papa still home?" Lisi didn't want to see him this morning.

"No, he left early."

"Good." Lisi stretched and rose out of bed only to stretch again. She spent half the night awake, worried about Lea, and the other half thinking about her papa. After he left last night, the three of them sat together for two hours in silence before Mrs. Hertz prayed. Just from being together they seemed to draw strength from each other and from God. It was only when their mama finished praying, stood up, and smoothed her skirt that she declared they all needed to be brave and to trust in God. She reminded them Lea was a smart girl, she would be all right. Lisi didn't think it was the right time to ask what being smart had to do with being lucky.

She noticed Rille still stood in the doorway watching her. "What's wrong?"

"Nothing." Rille shut the door and sat on her bed. "Don't worry about Papa, Lisi. Ever since the start of the war he's been like that to all of us, not just you."

"I know. Thanks for trying, but you don't have to. It doesn't matter."

"Do you remember when Henry enlisted?"

Lisi knew what Rille was doing and appreciated the effort. She nodded. "I don't think I've ever seen Papa so angry. Poor Henry, he felt so proud to finally made a decision that he thought would make Papa happy." Lisi remembered the way he waltzed into the kitchen as the family sat down to dinner and made his announcement. He had told them it wouldn't be much longer before Hitler would begin to show his true power. "Papa yelled so loudly that night. I saw Mama clean his hand after he banged it on the table. He didn't think anyone saw, but I did. Why did he get so angry, Rille?"

Rille winked. "I saw it too. That's not what hurt him, though. His hands were hurt before, and the banging only reopened old wounds." Rille saw the confusion on her sister's face but couldn't tell her about the conversation he had with their mama the night he came home injured.

"Papa was angry because Henry wasn't sixteen yet. At that time you had to be sixteen to enlist."

"So, Henry lied?"

"Henry lied. Don't think any less of him, Lisi. Lots of people have told little white lies during the war. He did it because he thought he was doing something good."

"I felt so sad for Mama. She just stood at the sink and cried and cried. She never said goodbye to him, Rille. What if he never...."

"Lisi, don't. Don't think like that. The war will be over soon, and you will see Henry again. I promise." Lisi knew Rille couldn't make a promise like that, but she let her sister hug her until their mama called for Lisi.

Clothes lay strewn across the floor from the night before, so Lisi threw the same ones on and ran a brush quickly through her hair. She felt the urgency of making the hour-long train ride to Wurzburg. After pulling her hair up, she padded down the stairs, anxious to find her mama.

"Lisi, there you are. Come on, Little One. We have to catch the morning train to Wurzburg. We are going to bring Lea home."

"Can I eat something first?" Her mama answered by offering a biscuit wrapped in cloth. Lisi knew what that meant. It meant she could eat once they were comfortably settled onto the train. Lisi didn't even look behind her as they walked out the door toward the station.

"How are we going to find her? Where is she?" Lisi settled into her seat and unfolded her napkin. Lea worked for a rich Nazi family in Wurzburg. Lisi assumed he was some sort of officer by the way her mama talked. She didn't see her sister often anymore, but when she did, Lea didn't talk much about her job. Everything Lisi knew her mama had told her.

"I have no idea, honey. I'm hoping she'll be home, but I wrote down the address of her job just in case." Mrs. Hertz rested her head against the seat and closed her eyes. *When did she get those lines around her eyes and mouth?* Lisi wondered as she studied the woman sitting next to her. The past few years the war took everyone's attention off the smaller, simpler things in life and only now, when Lisi had nothing else to do, did she really study her mama's face. It seemed like she was staring at a stranger sitting next to her. Lisi had been so wrapped up in her own life that she never really considered the effects of the war on her mama.

First, all three of her sons had left to fight in a war for a side she didn't believe in. Next, two of her daughters moved away. Finally, to top it off, she had to suffer the pain in watching her husband enjoy his life with others while she tried to maintain a good front for their family and friends. Lisi felt so sorry for her. She was all she had left at home right now.

The countryside rolled past as Lisi gazed out the window. When was the last time she stopped to admire the beauty of her country? The natural beauty, not Hitler's man-made beauty. For the remainder of the trip Lisi simply looked out the window and let her eyes soak in the beauty she beheld, grateful for the temporary escape from reality.

It seemed like only a few minutes had passed and Lisi felt a tap on her arm. "Lisi, wake up. We are in Scheinfeld." Lisi didn't have a chance to ask why they weren't in Wurzburg as her mama grabbed her hand and led her off the train. Thousands of people bustled along the platforms of the strange station. They all rushed, but nobody moved quickly. There was no room. Lisi was so busy watching everyone else she lost her mama's grip. "Little One!" Her mama shouted somewhere in front of her.

"Mama!" There! Lisi saw her just ahead by their next train. Steam poured from the engine as the whistle blew, warning passengers of the pending departure. Lisi tried to run but she had nowhere to go. As long as she kept her eyes on her mama she knew she would make it.

Her mama stepped up onto the second car back, her eyes on Lisi, watching her to make sure she made it. The whistle blew. Just a few yards left.

Slowly the train began to lurch forward. Her mama called her again, "Little One, hurry!" She was hurrying. Only a few more feet. She could make it. The train began to pick up speed and for the first time Lisi didn't think she would. Her tired legs slowed down when she felt large arms wrap around her little body and pick her up. Her mama began to cry as she was bounced closer to the train. The car was too far ahead, but a man from the car behind her mama saw what had happened and opened his window. Fortunately, the windows were large and Lisi, for once, felt grateful for her small size. Her rescuer lifted her up and pushed her through the window to a stranger on the other side. "Thank you, thank you, thank you." Her mama hugged the man. Lisi never saw who rescued her, but her mama told her later that it had been an American soldier. Lisi liked the Americans already.

Once settled onboard Lisi found out the reason they had to make the extra stop was because the damage from the bombings destroyed parts of the track, preventing the train from continuing along its usual route. The station in Wurzburg was just as crowded as Scheinfeld. "Everyone must have had the same idea we did," her mama remarked. They snaked their way across the platform and down the stairs to outside.

Once Lisi became accustomed to the mass crowd, she looked around. She couldn't believe it. "Mama!" Almost the entire city was leveled, in complete ruin.

"I know. Come on, this way."

A mix of emotions swirled through Lisi's body as the realization struck her how sheltered their small, secluded town was. So far. Sure, they had the air raids with the nights in the cellars, and the refugees, but they had been fortunate to miss this type of devastation. Even the most recent air raid produced nothing tangible for her to see. But here, buildings that once rose proud and majestic now stood as shells with their roofs torn off and windows blown out. Rubble covered entire streets. Lisi held her mama's hand so she wouldn't trip over anything.

After a lot of sidestepping and careful walking, they found Lea's apartment building. Thankfully she lived further from the center of town and her building had been one of the few that remained. "Lea!" Lisi ran to her sister, who stood outside the building. A suitcase sat next to her. She had a strange look in her eyes. They seemed almost lifeless.

When Lea heard her, she smiled and hugged first Lisi then their mama. A little bit of life returned to her face then. Mrs. Hertz scooped up the suitcase and with a simple "come," the three of them trekked back through the nightmare to the train station.

CHAPTER 18

April 1, 1945

The contrast of the bright April sunshine from the dark church felt good to Lisi as she stepped outside and breathed in the fresh spring air. Exhaling slowly, she lifted her head to the sun and took a moment to let the warm rays permeate her face. When you lived in a dominantly Catholic town, almost everyone attended Easter Sunday mass. Humming the tune to the last song the congregation sang, she stepped down into the large courtyard that covered the expanse of the church from end to end and strolled over to lean against the nearest tree.

Lisi loved people watching. She had a wealth of unnecessary information stored up in her brain, most of which she'd probably never need. Sometimes, though, it was a good thing. That's how she knew something had happened with Lea's job in Wurzburg. It was also how she knew Ruth needed her help when they first saw each other. Now, she watched Mr. and Mrs. Richter exit the church, arguing as usual. Gunther followed in uniform wearing his permanent scowl. Next came the Schmidts.

Lisi thought about Derrik and what Fritz had told her. She didn't know his family very well, but seeing his parents, Lisi had a feeling everything Fritz said was true.

Seeing Rose with her family made Lisi's stomach lurch. Why couldn't she say hello? She watched them stop to visit with friends. Oh, how she wished she could say something! When her family stepped outside, she saw Lea and forgot all about her friend.

Her sister, a true Aryan on the outside, not only with her blonde hair that fell in perfect waves, framing her slender face and long straight nose, but her eyes too. She had the brightest blue eyes anybody had ever seen. She didn't even need to smile and her eyes would sparkle. What really drew the boys to her was her slim frame that accentuated her long, lean legs.

Being ten years younger, Lisi admired her sister and considered her almost like a second mother when their mama had been too busy with other things. Since she moved to Wurzburg, though, the new job consumed all of Lea's time. Lisi thought it was so glamorous, but she could tell by the way Lea talked that she had a secret.

She thought about the other night when she tried to ask Lea about her job again. Lisi let the feel of the brush against her scalp sooth her. Lea was the best hair-brusher ever. "It's not that glamorous, Lisi. I clean their house, wash their clothes, and that's all."

That wasn't all, and Lisi knew it. She might have lived in a small town, but that didn't mean she was naive. She saw the pictures in the newspapers. Women flaunted their long, glittery dresses while they feasted on exquisite food.

She knew Lea was hiding something from her, but it never worried her until now.

Lisi watched her sister walk across the courtyard. Same posture, same facial expression she wore in Wurzburg at her apartment. It looked like defeat. The sparkle her eyes once possessed vanished. She may have been able to fool everyone else, but she couldn't fool her youngest sister.

Pushing away from the tree Lisi started to make her way toward Lea. Rille stood to the side talking with some friends, and she had no idea where her parents were. Halfway across the yard she halted as a young man in a crisp, clean Nazi uniform pushed passed her and paraded on a one-way path to her sister.

Ugh. Gunther. Of course. Who else had as rude manners as him? *It's Easter, for crying out loud. Honestly. Don't you guys get a day off from torturing civilians?* Gunther reached Lea and forced himself in her face with his womanizing smile and smooth ways.

No way was Lisi going to make her sister spend one more unbearable second with him. Besides, what would her husband, Johann, think when he returned from the war? She took a deep breath and smoothed her hair, then marched toward the couple. Just looking at his short, fat body made her think of a honey bear trying with all his might to climb the honey tree but never getting off the ground.

She was closing in fast, but so was he. Her heart pounded. What would she say when she got there? Go back to the rock you crawled out from? She wiped the sweat from her hands on her soft, red dress. She'd pay for that later when her mama saw, but she didn't care. The last thing she wanted was for Gunther Richter see her sweat.

Shouts came out of nowhere across the courtyard and stopped her dead in her tracks. She heard it too. The air raid siren. Where was the nearest shelter? It didn't matter. It was too late. "Defleegers!" Someone screamed out the name given to the P51 Mustang low-flying airplanes that held two machine guns, one in each wing. She stood cemented in place, her face stricken with terror as she tried to contemplate what to do. Should she run? Should she stay? All of a sudden, her mind blanked. She couldn't think. Fortunately, Lea ran from behind and grabbed Lisi's hand. "Defleegers!" she shouted again. Lisi used her sister's momentum and both girls started to run when someone pushed in between them. For an instant Lisi was alone. *Where had Lea gone? There!* She saw Lea stop and call her name, turning around in confusion between the mass of people running for shelter.

As the six planes dived in position, Lisi thought they were coming straight for her. She froze in her spot. "Lisi!" Lea called to her again.

Lisi snapped out of it when she heard her name and forced her feet to move. She knew the planes would shoot at any second. If she could only get to the safety of the trees at the end of the courtyard she'd be safe.

Two things happened. The planes began to fire their guns, causing complete mayhem and panic. At the same time Lisi felt herself pushed from behind and thrust to the ground under the weight of another body. She screamed until her lungs couldn't take the pressure.

Soon it became eerily quiet. Lisi's savior awkwardly pushed off her and, as she sat up, offered her his hand. She noticed the gray sleeve and her heart stopped. A Nazi soldier. According to the patches on the sleeve, someone rather important.

Lisi's mind reeled. Her safety had been placed in the hands of a Nazi solider. She hesitated. Should she accept his help? If she did, would she be indebted to him forever? If she didn't, was that some sort of crime? Out of instinct she grasped his hand. Whoever it was, underneath the gray uniform he was a person with a heart just like hers. She didn't need to be afraid of him.

He pulled her up so rapidly that she almost fell into him. She put her hand out to stop herself and it landed on his chest. "Danke." Thanking him, she quickly pulled herself as far away as possible and looked up so she could see her rescuer.

"Gunther!" She could feel her face burning, flushed from the humiliation.

"Well, if it isn't the little Hertz." Lisi could've punched him, standing there with that stupid smirk on his face. She knew he probably just saved her life. What's worse, he knew it, and she had no doubt he would use that against not only her but her entire family.

Struggling with words, Lisi excused herself to find her family. She raced as quickly as she could across the courtyard.

CHAPTER 19

Everyone celebrated Easter Sunday in a small Catholic town like theirs. Families typically gathered together to share a midday potluck. All that changed today, and instead most of the townspeople chose to stay in their own homes.

Lisi trailed behind her family on the walk home and went straight to her room to change her dress. It figured, of all the places to fall she had to fall on the one dirt patch with rocks. She inspected her dress closely. Not only was it covered in dirt but several holes made it look like large polka dots. She counted them. Six holes. One hole for each plane that attacked. Her eyes filled with tears as the weight of the war pressed against her heart. All she wanted was to change out of her dress and lie down until dinner.

As she opened the closet to look for another dress, she made a new song about the war. She sang about her brothers, she sang about her papa, she sang about Hitler, and she sang about all the people who called themselves Nazis. She even added a line about Ruth. Finding another dress, she pulled it roughly off the hook and turned to close her door. *Funny,* she thought, forgetting about her new war song, *the room seems so much brighter.* Murmuring about Rille leaving the light on again, Lisi checked and found it was off. *Odd,* she thought.

Something in her told her to look up. Light streamed in through the ceiling, and Lisi could make out the beautiful blue sky decorated with wisps of clouds floating overhead. Several holes penetrated the ceiling. She counted. Six. Just like the planes. Just like her dress. The realization hit her. The holes came from the machine guns of the fighter planes. If it had been only a few hours earlier she could have been in bed. Then, for some odd reason, she made a connection. Six planes, six holes in her dress, six holes in the ceiling. 666. Lea had taught her about the devil's number a long time ago. Thinking of everything she heard about Hitler and the names her papa called him, a thought began to form in her mind. Was Hitler the devil?

"Mama! Mama!" Lisi darted out of the room and practically tumbled down the stairs.

"Lisi, stop yelling this instant. What's this about?" Lisi pushed her way past her papa and ran right into her mama.

"Little One, what is it?" Lisi wrapped her arms around her and sobbed. "Tell me, now, what happened?" Her mama took her shoulders and gently pushed her away from her so she could see Lisi's face. Gently she wiped the tears from her daughter's eyes.

Lisi took a deep, shaky breath before she spoke. "Upstairs. The ceiling. Look!" Mr. Hertz took the lead while the rest of the family followed. Stopping in the hallway, he noticed more holes in the ceiling above the stairs. Upon further investigation, there were bullet holes in her parents' room too, but the boys' room had been spared. Ironically, the only room protected from gunfire was the vacant room, vacant because its three inhabitants currently fought against the attackers.

Later that evening, when the radio was turned on low and Lisi took up her post by the window, her mama walked by to get a drink in the kitchen. All through supper and the rest of the afternoon Lisi couldn't stop thinking about the triple sixes. It troubled her deeply and she wanted to talk to her mama about it, but the timing hadn't been right. Until now.

"Mama? Could I ask you something?" Lisi's eyes never left the road.

"What is it, Lisi?" Mrs. Hertz glanced toward the living room. Lisi knew she didn't want to miss anything that would be announced on the radio, but she couldn't get this out of her mind.

"It's about the attacks. And the whole war, really." She must've looked pathetic because her mama held up one finger, went to the kitchen for her Bible, and came back carrying a chair.

"Ok, Little One. Talk to me."

Lisi loved that she could talk to her mama about anything. She paused, needing a minute to organize her thoughts. "At church today when the planes flew by, I don't know why, but I counted them. There were six."

She waited, though she wasn't sure why. If she wanted a reaction from her mama, she didn't get anything other than tired eyes and a sweet smile.

"After we came home I noticed the holes in my dress and I don't know why but I counted them. There were six."

Lisi's mother still watched and waited, but her face showed a slight understanding of where this might be going.

"The holes in my ceiling...there were six." She paused for effect, waiting for the understanding to sink in. "Six. Six. Six." Each time she said the number, she gave her mama time to process it. "Six. Six. Six." Just in case her mama missed it the first time. She watched intently, searching for any hint of a reaction.

For a split second Lisi saw something flash across her mama's face, but then it vanished. "Little One, I think you read too much into things. This is merely a coincidence, that's all." Her voice sounded fake.

"Face it, Mama. You see it too." Lisi listened to herself as she said the word, "mama," and considered the irony in the context of their grown-up conversation. "Lea taught me all about the devil's number. Look around you. Admit it. It all makes sense."

Mrs. Hertz shook her head vigorously. "Stop it, child, you can be so dramatic sometimes. You're just looking for trouble."

"Don't call me 'child', and don't tell me to stop it. It's all right, Mama, I'm scared too. Fritz, Henry and Albert, what are they doing right now? Doing a monster's dirty work? And Lea had that awful job so she could feed herself while her husband also fights. They are all working for the devil!"

"Lisi, I said stop it!"

"No, Mama, I won't. This is his war and we are all his pawns whether we want to be or not! I hate Hitler and I hate what this country has become! I won't give in to him anymore! We're fighting on the wrong side, and the only reason England and France and America are fighting against us is because we started it!"

"Lisi! What is this about?" Sometime during her outburst her papa snuck up on her, which was almost impossible because he was so big. Now he listened to her carry on like a little child. So much for acting like a *backfisch.*

"Nothing." Pushing past him Lisi grabbed her sweater that hung by the door and stormed out of the house. There was only one place she wanted to be. With Rose. Rose would understand. Wouldn't she? Ruth would understand for sure, but Lisi knew her family was sharing Easter supper with Father Alder and a few other refugee families. Unperturbed that it was Easter night and curfew was quickly approaching, she ran across the yard. She'd pay for it later, but she didn't care. Right now she needed to talk to Rose.

Knocking on her neighbors' door, Lisi stood, shaking. Gratefully, Rose opened the door. "Lisi, what are you doing outside?" She yanked her friend into the house and shut the door quickly but as quietly as she could.

Turning to face her friend again, Rose asked in a loud whisper. "My mama is just in the other room. What is going on? Why are you...." She stopped and held out her arms to Lisi. "What's wrong, my friend?"

Lisi shook with violent sobs as she cried in her best friend's arms, thankful she was still welcome even with the change in their relationship. A few minutes of weeping were all Lisi had right now for years of pain and loss. She let Rose lead her into the kitchen and sit her at the table with a hot cup of acorn coffee. She took a sip then puckered her lips at the taste of the weaker, unappealing coffee substitute. "Now, talk to me."

Lisi explained how the day's events unfolded. Rose listened without interrupting much, only an "oh" here and there. When Lisi finished talking about the holes in the roof, Rose spoke. "You poor thing. We were already on our way home, so we were able to get to the Berger's shelter. Once we came home Mama inspected and found nothing had been harmed. I'm so sorry it was so much worse for you."

Reassured by the words, Lisi decided to finish. Surely Rose's salute and more frequent interactions with the other kids at school didn't mean all that they appeared to mean. "That's not all." As Lisi told the rest of her story, finishing with the realization that maybe this was, in fact, the devil's war, Rose's expression changed. "What's the matter? Don't you agree with me? Look around you. This is hell."

"Lisi, I...." Rose was interrupted by her mama who came in for a drink of water.

"Oh, hello Lisi. What brings you here at this time of day? Are your parents all right?" Mrs. Meyer's face transformed from surprise to pleasantness to a dark look of worry.

"Hello, Mrs. Meyer. Yes, they are all right, thank you. I was just, um, upset about something and really needed to talk to Rose. It couldn't wait for school tomorrow. I'm sorry to have bothered you." Lisi stood to leave, but Mrs. Meyer waved her hand at her.

"No worry. I will walk you home when you are finished as long as your parents know where you are. Go ahead, I won't interrupt you girls anymore. I was just talking to Gretel about how fortunate we are to have such a strong group of men to protect our country. We know how difficult it has been on you and your family with the boys gone. Well, I'll give you a couple of minutes." Mrs. Meyers sped up her words and hurried out of the kitchen.

"Mama really misses Papa. We haven't heard from him in weeks."

Lisi nodded, staring at her friend. Rose lowered her eyes, unwilling to meet her gaze. "Rose." Lisi let her name linger in the air until she looked up. Lisi was definitely the leader of the two and on numerous occasions during their friendship she took on the role of a parent-like figure while Rose settled back as the less confrontational child. "The salute. Did you really mean it? Do you support Hitler?" She already knew the answer by the look on Rose's face. "Are you hoping Hitler will still win this war? After six long years, what they've done to our families, our friends." The last word was whispered, and she found she couldn't go on. Since Rose had only sisters, she didn't fully understand the effects the war had on Lisi's family.

"Lisi, you don't understand. It's not like that. My family doesn't support Hitler. We support Germany. It's our home. But we respect Hitler. We know he's trying to make our country great again." Her words sounded shallow, and she knew it.

"Respect? Rose, do you remember Sara? And Joseph? And all the others? Have you forgotten? Because there isn't a night I don't see them in my dreams."

Sitting up straighter, Rose looked Lisi right in the eye. "Do you ever think maybe Hitler was on to something? Maybe there really WAS something wrong with them. Charles Darwin created it. Adolf Hitler only followed. It's like when Frau Zott teaches us something new at school. We trust her, so we take the new information and use it. Survival of the fittest. Those of us who survived, well, maybe we are superior to those that did not. I don't know, Lisi, but just think about it. It sounds logical, right?" Lisi's eyes widened at each sentence as they sounded crazier and crazier. She had a sudden urge to leave. She couldn't be here anymore. Here, in her second home, her eyes opened to the filthy truth of what had become of this war. The tapestry was now completely ripped open.

"I need to go." Lisi pushed back from the table knocking her chair over without even hearing it. She fled out the door before Mrs. Meyer could slip her feet into her shoes and raced home without any care to the dangers that might be lurking in the twilight shadows around her. Was it any more dangerous than what had been happening in broad daylight right in front of her?

Running up to her door, she pushed the handle and shoved her shoulder into the door, but it wouldn't open. She tried the handle again to no avail. Not caring who was around, Lisi banged on the door. Shadows danced as headlights approached the bend just down the road. Lisi began to feel the ramifications of her stupid childish actions and banged harder and louder.

As the headlights lit up the front of her house, the door flew opened and shut just as quickly. Lisi found herself sprawled across the floor. She looked up to see her papa looming over her, scowling. She felt like a mouse caught floating in a pitcher of milk. Slowly, she stood and thought about running upstairs and locking her door for a hundred years.

She tried an alternative tactic. Kindness. "Thank you for opening the door, Papa." No response. Another tactic. Naiveté. "It must've gotten stuck somehow."

"I locked it. Only someone as stupid as a little child would be out at dark during a war."

You go out every night, she thought.

"You are never to go out after dark again. Do you understand?" He didn't wait for a response. He stormed upstairs and locked himself in his room. It was early. Too early. He never went to bed until he finished listening to the radio program, and it was too early for it to be over. Lisi looked at her mama in the living room near the silent radio, waiting for the car to drive by outside. She looked at Rille who stood by the window.

Good. Let someone else do her job for once. She stood slowly and looked at her mama once more before retiring to bed. She knew by the look on her mama's face that she wanted to hug her and tell her it would be all right, that she wasn't mad at her. She also knew her mama wouldn't do that with her papa home.

Lisi turned and tiptoed up the stairs by herself, extra careful not to make any sound. In her room Lea was already undressing for the night. Lisi noticed the potato sacks that had been tacked up across the ceiling until her papa could repair the roof in the morning. She crawled into bed without changing her clothes and fell right asleep.

Groaning, Lisi pulled the covers over her head and rolled over. Was it so much to ask for a few more minutes of sweet sleep before rising to get dressed for school? Apparently so. *Why does the sun have to rise this morning?* she thought. *There is nothing to be sunny about today.* It was Monday, and the sun was annoyingly bright as it shone through the makeshift cover of her ceiling, welcoming a new day.

Since the blankets still didn't keep the sun's glory out, Lisi plopped the pillow over her head and prayed that some sort of strange, incurable illness would quickly consume her body. This way she wouldn't have to face the day, the week, the month. Thinking about last night, Lisi felt sick at the idea of seeing Rose at school today. Actually, Lisi felt sick at facing anyone. Except Ruth. Ruth seemed to be the only one Lisi could talk to about her own fears.

CHAPTER 20

Rose seemed more distant than ever. For the past two weeks Lisi hadn't seen her at all other than at school, and then she always averted her eyes. It was a Saturday afternoon and the rain poured down on the town, forming large pools on the dirt road. Lisi sat at the window and moped. Mesmerized by one particular pool, she stared as it slowly expanded. Was God crying? Did He cry for her? Lisi doubted it. Why would He waste tears on her?

The empty roads mirrored the loneliness Lisi felt inside. A single, foolish figure dashed past her house, their rain gear offering no protection whatsoever. Then, out of nowhere, another figure appeared from behind and caught up to the first. Side by side the pair hurried down the road, disappearing around a bend.

Lisi's heart felt heavy. She remembered a time not too long ago when she and Rose danced in the rain together, laughing and singing as if they performed for the entire town. At least until both their mamas dropped the curtain on their performance.

For some reason that memory struck a chord in her mind. It was time to make up. She missed her best friend. She hated the way things had become, hated seeing Rose at school, and she especially hated seeing her with her new friends. Did it really matter if they had different beliefs? They could agree to disagree, right? Maybe?

The rain subsided and Lisi knew it was time. She opened the door and stepped outside at the same time she saw Rose leave her own house. Someone else approached Rose's house and stopped in front of her. Lisi pressed herself behind her door. Good thing nobody else was home right now. Otherwise she'd get a scolding for keeping the door open.

Lisi watched as Rose and the stranger briefly talked. It seemed like the person wanted Rose to go with her, but Rose refused. Lisi heard angry voices before the girl stormed away. Second guessing her decision, Lisi shrank back inside her house.

"Lisi?" The question in Rose's voice resembled the questions swirling in Lisi's mind.

"Oh, hi, Rose." She peered around her door. No going back now. "I was just going to come over. I, uh...."

"I was just going to come and see you too. I miss you, Lisi. I know we might not agree on everything, but is there any way we can overlook all that and be friends again?"

Lisi slumped against her door, her muscles weak with relief. "Best friends?"

"Is there anything else?" Both girls stepped into the street and met halfway between houses for a hug.

The rain picked up again but it didn't matter. Lisi and Rose didn't even hear it as they helped Mrs. Hertz, Lea and Rille prepare dinner. "Did you finish your mathematics, Rose? I can't seem to figure out the last problem."

Rose laughed. "Some things never change. Yes, I did finish it." Lisi looked expectantly, waiting. "Go get it. I'll help you." Just like old times. Lisi ran from the kitchen and up to her room.

Homework in hand, Lisi was on her way back to the kitchen when she heard a soft knock on her door. She froze. The knock sounded familiar. Lisi didn't need to open the door to know who stood on the other side. Her stomach somersaulted. She had forgotten her plans with Ruth. Would Rose accept Lisi and Ruth's friendship?

"Hi." Lisi slowly opened the door and Ruth wrapped her arms around her friend. Lisi didn't return the hug. "What's wrong?" Lisi checked the kitchen doorway. Good, she heard Rose in the kitchen with her family. "Lisi, what is it?"

Ugh, what was she doing? She had reverted back to the old Lisi. No, she would not become her again. She took a deep breath. "Hi, Ruth. Nothing's wrong, I just forgot we had plans. Sorry." That sounded lame, even to her. No, she needed to be honest. "Actually, that's not entirely true. You see, Rose...."

"Lisi?" Rose appeared in the doorway.

"Hi, Rose." Ruth's voice remained pleasant. The world stopped for what seemed like hours to Lisi. Then the most unexpected thing happened. She watched Rose slowly walk toward Ruth, and for a brief moment she thought she would shove her right out the door. Instead, Rose grabbed Ruth with both arms and pulled her into a tight embrace.

"I'm sorry, Ruth, for the way I've treated you. Can you forgive me?" Rose held tightly as she apologized.

Would Ruth forgive her? Lisi held her breath. Finally, Ruth lifted her arms and hugged Rose too. "There's nothing to forgive."

CHAPTER 21

"Hurry up, Lisi. We're gonna be late and I'll get in trouble again." Lisi couldn't help it. It felt good to finally laugh with Rose again. She laughed so hard she stumbled over every rock and twig through Rose's field.

"Lisi! Come on!" Rose spun around causing wisps of dark hair to fall free of the pins that held the loose bun. Lisi laughed harder. Frustrated, Rose grabbed her hand and dragged her toward the edge of the field. Unfortunately, Rose was too busy looking at Lisi and missed the big rock until it was too late. They both tumbled to the ground and Rose finally succumbed to the laughter.

"Why are you always so worried? You know they will save you some food. They always do."

"Mama says if I'm late to the table one more time I won't be able to see you for three days. And what would I do then?"

Rose stood and pulled Lisi to her feet. She had just caught her balance when a blaring siren filled the air. "Air raid siren!" the girls shouted in unison. Lisi stood dumbfounded. It was the middle of the day. Air raids usually came during the night, while she slept in her own home with her family, not in a wide open space in her friend's field.

"To the woods, girls! To the woods!" Mrs. Meyer ran out from the barn.

Frozen to her spot, Rose didn't seem to hear her mama, but Lisi heard. "Come on, Rose, let's go!" Grabbing Rose's hand, Lisi pulled her toward the tree line. Thankfully Rose's feet moved even if nothing else in her body worked.

It didn't take Mrs. Meyer long to catch up. Lisi seemed surprised at how fast she could run. They looked up in unison and saw planes overhead. Lisi knew what that meant, and it wasn't good. She focused her eyes on one giant tree trunk in a spot that had been carved out. She would keep her eyes on that spot and pray they made it.

True to her nature, Lisi stayed strong until she burst through the front door of her home. She wasn't sure if her family still hid next door in the shelter or not. Overcome by the comforting aroma of bread baking and the sound of the radio playing in the other room, she began to sob as she stumbled past Rilli at the window and into the living room where her family listened to the voice that boomed from the little box.

"Mama, Mama, Mama!" She couldn't say anything else.

Met by angry faces and "shhs" by her sisters, Lisi looked to her mama. Leaping from the couch, she wrapped her arms around Lisi. "Shh, hush now Lisi. It's all right.

You are safe now. We are all safe and that is what matters. Please don't cry. We must be quiet now. We are waiting for a special announcement. Come, sit with me."

"What announcement, Mama?" Lisi whispered so she wouldn't aggravate her papa.

Mrs. Hertz put her finger to her mouth and smiled at Lisi. She would have to wait for the announcement. For the moment, until further notice from her papa, a ban had been placed on talking.

CHAPTER 22

May 2, 1945

The radio played quietly in the living room as Lisi finished clearing the dinner dishes. Her papa had rushed home from work earlier that evening and immediately turned on the radio. He said he heard a rumor. Nothing more.

Now, with the table cleared, Lisi joined her family in the living room. Settling herself onto the floor beside the couch, she smoothed out her dress as they waited. Ever since the big announcement a couple of days ago that Adolf Hitler committed suicide with his girlfriend, Eva Braun, everyone in the country held their breath, waiting for the end. Finally, the news they longed for had been revealed.

Mr. Hertz looked at Lisi and tipped his head toward the window. She didn't think it was necessary, anymore, with Hitler dead, but since her papa gave her the silent treatment tonight, she figured she'd obey without arguing. The radio announced that Soviet troops had marched in and captured Berlin. All the soldiers had been ordered to put their weapons down.

"Dear God, don't let the Soviets reach us first."

Even Mr. Hertz looked like he was praying as he switched off the radio, and Lisi returned to the living room. "What is so bad? What does this mean, Mama?"

"It means we better pray really hard tonight that the Americans reach us before the Soviets," Lea answered.

"They are worse than Hitler. They're monsters. They hurt women and children."

"That's enough, Rille." Mrs. Hertz interrupted. "Let's just pray the Americans are close." Lisi closed her eyes and prayed.

CHAPTER 23

May 7, 1945

Lisi linked arms with Rose and Ruth as the trio walked down the street to school. She knew it would be a good day. The promise of an end to the war, her papa had been away again, and she and her sisters seemed to be getting along better than ever. The sun was shining, and Lisi felt the warmth on her face. No Soviets had entered their town yet, so she took that as a good sign. Yes, winter was over and spring had come, just like her mama said.

As they entered the center of town, Lisi noticed a change in the atmosphere. She had developed a talent for ignoring most of the soldiers' comments and jests, especially the soldiers she knew, but this morning to her surprise there was none of that. They remained in their duties but wore downcast expressions. Some had red, blotchy faces. Those soldiers ignored the girls. A few of them smiled at the girls or raised their hand in a Nazi salute, but not in the strong way they used to.

It all seemed so different, but Lisi wouldn't find out why until the next day.

CHAPTER 24

May 8, 1945, VE Day

When Lisi woke up Tuesday morning she had no idea what the day would hold. The noise from the radio drifted up the stairs. On her way by, she stopped in the doorway to the living room. Her parents huddled around the radio. Her sisters stood nearby too, listening. Nobody stood at the window. They stared at the radio as if they expected the speaker to jump out himself. What was so important?

"Mama?"

The voice of her daughter startled Mrs. Hertz so much she let out a cry, which annoyed her husband. "Lisi, you scared me. We are waiting for a special report."

"About what?"

"Can you two just be quiet?" Mr. Hertz snapped.

Welcome home, Papa. "I have to go." Lisi couldn't wait to get out of the house. She didn't care about the special report. She could find out later. The war had to end soon. She didn't know how much more she could take of her papa's anger and bitterness. She would later regret those thoughts when she wondered if she would ever see him again.

On the way to school Lisi noticed even more of a difference than yesterday. The air seemed lighter. A dark, imaginary cloud lifted from over the town, and she wasn't sure why. Only later when she and Rose passed Mr. Richter's office on their way to pick up Ruth and Peter did they find out why. A loudspeaker radio had been erected in the center of town. News of the Allies' victory blared from it. First in German, then the same announcement in a language Lisi didn't recognize.

Mr. Richter stood outside in front of his office surrounded by a group of people. As they walked by the air still felt heavy and almost dark here. *Anywhere Mr. Richter goes, he brings a dark cloud with him,* Lisi thought to herself as she noticed him speak to the group before walking toward them. Lisi tried to speed up, but not fast enough.

"Good morning, Lisi."

"Good morning, Mr. Richter." Lisi continued to walk toward Ruth's house.

"Good morning Rose. It is a good day, girls, no? The war is over and we can finally move on with our lives. Lisi, tell your mama and papa I said hello." Then he turned and walked away.

The girls stood dumbfounded and stared after him. A group of Allied soldiers approached, and Lisi gripped Rose's hand. Where they were from? Were they Soviet?

American? Mr. Richter smiled and greeted them as they walked by but only received nasty looks in return. The two girls forgot about Ruth and Peter. They turned and ran in the opposite direction taking the long way to school that day.

CHAPTER 25

Later that afternoon, Lisi sat with Rose and Ruth on their favorite bench down the road from Lisi's house. A compilation of twisted tree limbs, one of her Jewish neighbors created it when Lisi was little. This particular day turned out to be unusually warm for May. The sweat found its path and slowly made its way down Lisi's face until it hung from her chin. Dipping her head down, she waited patiently for it to fall into the pool between her feet. A curl of her sunset red hair flopped into her eyes. She let out a breath aimed upward, knowing the lock would flop right back.

The earlier news of the victory of the Allies caused a sense of relief to sweep through the small town. The radio announced that early yesterday the Nazi army surrendered officially. Today would come to be forever known as VE Day, or Victory in Europe Day. Mrs. Zott had informed her class that it was the Americans who invaded their town, and they rejoiced.

Already several neighbors stopped to celebrate with the girls as they walked by to find friends and family.

For many, it didn't matter that Germany lost the war. The relief of the end far outweighed everything else. For now. Despite the heat, it was a good day. "Do you think Ludwig will come over to see me when he gets home?"

"Rose Meyer, you're ridiculous!" Lisi laughed and turned her attention from her sweat to her friend. Wiping her face, she peeled herself off the wooden bench and stepped onto the road. Ludwig Fischer was fifteen and didn't know Rose existed, other than one day last year when he greeted her on the road with a "Heil Hitler" salute and a wink as he walked by.

"What? I'm just wondering." She held her palms up and shrugged her shoulders, then looked to her other friend. "Come on, Ruth. You can't tell me you don't want to meet him?"

"No way! I'm sure he can't even compare to Peter!"

Lisi and Rose laughed. "You're right, Ruth. He doesn't. But I still believe Lisi has a dirty little secret about that. And I'd rather think about the...."

"Think about the what?" Lisi looked up at her friend's stiff body. Her back was turned so she couldn't see Rose's fearful expression. "Fritz? Henry? Albert?" Lisi jumped up next to Rose, then Ruth followed. What she saw was not her brothers. Fear gripped her by the throat so intensely that she instinctively put her hands up in an attempt to tear it off. An army jeep led a caravan of army trucks. One thought gripped her, even though she knew it couldn't be true. It was the same thought that hovered over her family like a dark ghost waiting to attack, making its presence known but never letting on when the attack will come. *The Soviets.*

Seized with terror the three friends stood in the middle of the dirt road, arms linked. As the caravan approached, Lisi could see more clearly. The jeep held three soldiers, two in front, one in the back. They weren't Nazi trucks, Lisi knew that for sure. As much as those trucks frightened her, these unknown ones did so even more.

The soldier behind the wheel of the lead truck saw them, and Lisi thought she saw a slight smile cross his face as the jeep stopped directly in front of them.

The backseat soldier climbed down and inspected them. He did not smile. "Is this the home of Otto Hertz?" Painted on the front of the jeep in white letters were the words, "US Army." American soldiers! Relief washed over Lisi like a fresh rain only to freeze by icy fear as the two words she understood were those of her papa's name. *Why were American soldiers here looking for her papa?*

"Can you hear, or are you deaf? Does Otto Hertz live here?" The young soldier's lack of the German language told Lisi he hadn't been in Germany for very long. Unable to understand exactly what he said, she could tell by his tone that he wasn't looking for friendly conversation.

"Come on, Jimmy, they're just girls." The driver stood up and stepped out of the car to open the passenger doors. Turning to the girls, he flashed another smile that somehow stole all the words from Lisi's mouth. The solider in the passenger seat stepped out and filled the silence as he spoke in perfect German.

"Hello, we are looking for a carpenter to work at our barracks just outside of town. We were told Otto Hertz is the one we should speak to. Does he live here?"

Pointing to the house down the street, Rose answered. "Otto Hertz lives there. And this is his daughter, Lisi." Hearing Rose's terrified voice snapped Lisi back to reality. She could have hit her friend, and she would have if she hadn't been too scared to move. It didn't matter because Rose grabbed Ruth's hand, and the two of them walked away as fast as they could.

Great! If I ever get out of this alive, I need to find some new friends. Lisi stood, one solitary person to face what seemed like a legion of foreign soldiers. Bravely, she swallowed and lifted her chin high. "I am Lisi Hertz. My father is Otto Hertz. Please, come with me." The interpreter relayed her message to the arrogant man named Jimmy. Turning toward the house, she led three American soldiers into her German home.

CHAPTER 26

"Mama? Papa?" Lisi cracked the door just enough to peek her head inside. How could she prepare her parents for who was about to enter her home?

"Otto Hertz?" The sound of soldier Jimmy's voice breathed down her neck. It startled Lisi so much that she shut the door on her finger. She bit her bottom lip as tears sprang to her eyes from the pain. She took a deep breath, blinked, and opened the door.

"What's this?" Mr. Hertz's voice boomed into the foyer. "Who are you, and what are you doing in my home?"

Funny, Lisi always considered the Americans allies until this very moment. Everything she heard on the radio about them seemed so positive as they defeated Hitler and their promise of peace. Right now, though, well, this was different. The display she saw today in the street, and now, standing here in her small foyer like two stone statues that towered over her papa's five feet four inches, these boys playing men revealed nothing of the peaceful rewards of having the Americans in her country. It probably didn't help either that Jimmy reminded Lisi of the devil Hitler reincarnated, with his dark hair and minuscule mustache above his lip.

"Otto Hertz." Even with the American accent Lisi heard her papa's name as statement, not a question. Jimmy pressed on. "We are in need of a carpenter. Are you a Nazi?"

The interpreter took no more than a few seconds before Mr. Hertz shot back. "Am I a Nazi? That's none of your business! Now get out of my house!"

"Otto Hertz, I am asking you one more time by the authority of the American Army, are you a Nazi?"

"No," his voice gruff and low.

"Good. Then we're going to need you to come with us now, Sir."

Mr. Hertz stood taller as he replied to their command in German. "I may not be a Nazi, but it doesn't mean I trust you. I am not moving from my house until you tell me where you are taking me." Lisi examined her mama's movements as she stepped forward and clutched her husband's arm tightly. For being such a strong woman, Lisi had never seen her mama this scared.

"By order of the American army, you will come with us." Jimmy reached out to grab his other arm. Feeling helpless, Lisi let out a cry and moved herself in front of her papa to protect him. How silly she must have looked! She realized that too late, but what else could she do? Any other day she would have never gotten this close to him, but for some reason the fear of this situation outweighed any issues that existed between her and her papa.

"Move, Lisi." Standing tall, Otto Hertz placed his hand over his wife's for a brief moment and stepped forward to meet whatever future awaited him.

CHAPTER 27

The tiny foyer seemed vast after Jimmy and her papa left. "I'm sorry if we scared you, ma'am." The good-looking soldier put his hand to his hat as he addressed Mrs. Hertz. His German was broken but understandable. "He will be home tonight." Turning his head to Lisi, he smiled and walked out the door.

Too afraid to move, Lisi continued to stare at the wooden door, fists clenched so tightly she could feel her nails digging into the palms of her hands. Her mama released a huge sigh and she turned to look at her. What happened? Seconds ago her mama stood tall and brave as she watched the soldiers take her husband. Now, hunched over, she looked small and sad, like she had aged ten years. A single tear overflowed her left eye and trickled down her cheek.

Lisi went to her mama and wrapped her arms around her small middle. "He will be all right, Little One," her mother reassured her. Maybe the words were meant to reassure them both. Either way, they did little to calm the jitters Lisi felt.

"How do you know?" Lisi challenged as she pulled away. "How do you know for sure they will bring him back tonight? And how do you know they won't do anything to harm him? You don't know. You say these words, but you don't know!"

Surprise flashed across her mama's face. In truth she also surprised herself. Where did these feelings come from? Did she really care about what happened to her papa deep down inside? Her mama answered her. "Lisi, stop it. What is this? I have to believe that he will be all right and he will come home safely to us. If not, what kind of love is that? And what faith do I have then?"

"Love? You talk about love. What kind of love has he shown you lately? That touch he gave you on your hand was the first time I've seen him touch you since the war started."

"Lisi," Mrs. Hertz tried to interrupt, but Lisi was on a roll now and she wasn't about to quit. The mix of emotions that bottled up inside her surfaced from somewhere deep down, somewhere she didn't know. Anger, sadness, bitterness and fear all mixed into this terrible outburst.

As she continued, she knew she should stop, and she knew she should feel sorry for her mama. She did feel sorry for her, but right now she couldn't seem to control the words. If she didn't get them out, they might retreat back to that dark place inside her. "And," she continued, not giving her mama the chance to interrupt her, "this faith. Some days I wonder. Really wonder. Where is God? You talk about Him like He always hears you. Maybe He picks and chooses what He wants to hear. If He heard you, would He let Papa treat us like we are all one big mistake in his life? And if He heard you, do you really think He would have let this monster, this devil, rise up and murder all those innocent people? Half of our neighbors, Mama, dragged out of their beds, leaving everything, and we may never see them again."

Anger replaced Lisi's sadness. She thought that if she said all those things out loud it would help her feel better, that it would take away the pain she felt, but it didn't. The pain was still real, and now she felt guilty too for what she said to her mama. One thing she managed to keep inside, however, was the fact that no matter how she felt about her papa, she couldn't wait until tonight for his return.

CHAPTER 28

Lisi sat with her face pressed against the kitchen window, as she had done for the last two hours, watching and waiting. Her mama sat with Lea and Rille at the table listening to the small radio fill the room with information on the victory over the Nazi army. It was such a relief to be free from the responsibilities of window guard, and yet here she sat watching for another truck. She didn't really care about what the announcer said. It sounded like the same stories from the past week, ever since the Russians invaded Berlin and the Germans in Italy surrendered.

Yet for some reason her mama couldn't pull herself away. Turning from the window, Lisi sighed. "It's starting to get dark. Supper's over. Where is he? They said they would bring him home tonight. Right? Isn't that what the soldier said? Maybe we misunderstood him. Maybe he said, 'we are not sorry, but since we now have control of your country, we are going to take your papa prisoner and chop off his hands.'"

"Lisi, you're being very dramatic. Come, sit down and listen. It's all very exciting news. Papa will be home when they are finished." Lea patted the seat next to her.

At that moment headlights shone through the window and tires bumped over the rocks in the road. All four girls jumped up at the same time and raced to the door.

Lisi reached it first and wasted no time flinging it wide open. The jeep had only just approached their house. For an instant she feared it might be the Soviets, but that was silly. She ran down the step and stopped at the side of the street. The kind soldier drove, and the soldier named Jimmy sat in the backseat. The jeep came to a stop in front of where Lisi stood and the driver turned off the motor.

Sitting in the passenger seat, Mr. Hertz smiled. She had forgotten he had teeth. How handsome he had been. She could see why her mama fell in love with him. He opened the door and stepped onto the street holding papers in his hand as the driver came around the front of the car to stand next to him. Lisi couldn't help herself. She ran to her papa and threw her arms around his waist. "Papa!" *He's safe,* was all she kept thinking.

She longed for his love then. As he placed his hands on her shoulders she began to feel the pain melt away but just as quickly he pushed her away from him. "Lisi, please. Enough." He walked toward the house, past her sisters, past her mama, who stood in the doorway, waiting. Lisi wiped a tear away and prayed the soldier didn't see. No such luck, though, and she felt a gentle hand on her shoulder quite the opposite of the other hand she just felt.

"Guten abend." Wow. The American attempted to speak her language. Maybe he wanted to be friends with her family. After all, he brought her papa home, hadn't he? Looking up at him, he extended his right hand to Lisi. Not in a "Heil Hitler" salute kind of way but in a "nice to meet you" kind of way. She discreetly wiped another stray tear, angry at herself for getting this upset, and extended her right hand to grasp his. "My name is Jerry." He patted his free hand against his chest.

"Lisi." The officer's hand was warm and twice the size of hers, but it felt comfortable. Secure. Safe.

"Lisi." He let the name roll off his tongue. "Nice to meet you. Your papa's a great guy. He really helped us out today." Lisi stood wide-eyed at this American soldier speaking German. Jerry laughed at her surprise. "I've been teaching myself as soon as I knew I was coming here. Figured it might come in handy sometime. Anyway, the barracks we're in are in great need of repair. Your papa offered to help us fix them." Then he chuckled. "Well, he didn't exactly offer. We came into town looking for a carpenter and were told your papa is the best around."

Lisi understood most of what he said. "So I've heard." The statement came out drenched in sarcasm.

Jerry understood and, in an attempt to soothe things over, he offered a peace agreement. "I'm sorry we barged into your house like we did before. You must have been very scared. I want you to know we will not do anything to eat your papa. We will take great care of him."

For the first time Lisi laughed. "I think you mean you won't do anything to hurt him."

Jerry laughed at his error. "I guess I still have work to do. Anyway, if we are going to see your papa every day, I'd like to be friends. Maybe you can teach me more German?"

Lisi stared at this foreigner who had invaded her town and her life in one day. Could she trust him? Could she trust them? Were they really here to help her country, or would they do exactly what Hitler did? She was afraid, but at the same time something in the man's eyes revealed a genuine care and concern.

She shrugged her shoulders in response to her thoughts. Why not? The Americans couldn't be any worse than the Nazi army, so why not let her guard down a little and trust him? "Sure. Why not?"

Jerry smiled wide and popped his head inside the open door to her house. After bidding her parents farewell, he and Jimmy climbed into the car. Jerry waved to Lisi. She raised her hand to wave back when Jimmy scolded Jerry. Whatever he said, it wasn't nice, and Lisi had a feeling it had to do with her. She lowered her hand and quickly hid it behind her back.

CHAPTER 29

The summer of 1945 brought talk around town of the changes. A strange feeling filled the air, and townspeople hadn't yet decided how they felt about the American control. Supposedly they were much better than the Russians, but not all Americans turned out as nice as Jerry. Neighbors talked about the mean things soldiers said to them or their children. The taunts went both ways, however, when the colored American soldiers patrolled the streets.

Lisi watched as her papa happily settled into his new job. The first night he brought paperwork home to complete, and Lisi wondered about the truth of his answers. She overheard her parents talking in the kitchen.

"Anika, they are giving me almost double the ration cards because of this job. I'm not going to give them anything to hold against me."

"But, Otto, I remember when they bombed Wurzburg. I saw your face. You were very worried. How can you say it didn't affect you?"

"Yes, but I was only concerned for Lea's safety. I didn't lose one minute of sleep for anyone else. They don't need to know my feelings."

Most of the questions asked on the Fragebogen were created to denazify the Germans and mold them into what the Americans wanted. Since her papa wasn't a Nazi, why did this questionnaire make him so upset?

Lisi began to see the benefits of the end of the war. With the extra ration cards, her family had a little extra food to eat. Jerry started eating Sunday meals with them, and sometimes he would bring friends. Most of the time they ate dumplings with potatoes and gravy, Lisi's favorite.

During their third meal together, Lisi asked Jerry a question. "Shori, why aren't all the American soldiers nice to us like you are?" Most of Lisi's family had trouble pronouncing his name when they first met, so this became his nickname.

"Well, I hate to say it, but many of them think they're better than everyone else. They think they need to fix what went wrong here with Hitler by changing everyone. To them, all Germans are Nazis."

"But you don't think that. Can't you tell them?"

"Oh, I do, but I have to be very careful. You see, there is a rule that we aren't supposed to talk to any Germans unless it's part of our job. If I tell too many people about you, they will accuse me of being a Nazi sympathizer and I will be in big trouble."

"Then why do you come for supper every week? Is it so you can teach me more of your Frank Sinatra songs and dancing bugs?"

Jerry couldn't help laughing. The lines around his eyes crinkled when he looked at Lisi. "That's definitely a top priority. Hey, how's your jitterbug coming, anyway?"

"Jitterbug, dancing bug, whatever. Stop trying to change the subject. Why do they allow you to come here if it's against the rules? And my jitterbug is coming along fine."

Jerry looked toward Mr. Hertz. "Well, for one thing your papa has been a great help to our barracks. But it is also because your mama is considered vulnerable, and we are permitted to help people who are vulnerable."

Mrs. Hertz looked at her husband and shook her head. Another stretched response on the questionnaire. "What's vulnerable?" Lisi still didn't understand.

Mrs. Hertz replied, "It means I need help."

Jerry stepped in. "It means your mama has gone through a lot of stress and anxiety. Three of her children have been gone for a long time, and she doesn't know where they are or if they are alive. Two of her daughters lived in a city that fell under attack." Jerry glanced at Lea and Rille. Lisi realized that her papa hadn't been completely honest on his questionnaire. If Jerry knew, he didn't let it show. "So, because of those reasons, I was given special permission. Don't worry. These rules always change. Soon I will be able to visit any time I like! And then I will have more time to teach you the latest

American songs." He winked at her. Jerry knew how much she loved to sing. Lisi blushed.

The ban remained in effect until October 1, which made it very difficult whenever Lisi ran into Jerry on the street. He smiled and waved like he did to all the people in town, except when he was working. Then he looked so mean. Lisi knew he called it acting, but she looked forward to Sundays as much as her family did.

The first Sunday in July Jerry brought two soldiers with him from the barracks. Lisi had never seen them before. Lea opened the door for them, and Lisi clenched her teeth as Jerry flirted with her sister. Why didn't she mention her husband?

"Hey, Little One." Finally, Jerry noticed her. She felt like his pet dog as he patted her head and handed her his usual treat. This made Lisi angry. Why did he have to treat her like a little girl? She looked forward to Sundays, not just because of the special chocolate and chewing gum he brought her but because she could see him. Taking a deep breath, she forced herself to calm down. She wouldn't let anything get in her way today.

"Hey, Shori."

Jerry pecked Mrs. Hertz's cheek and introduced his friends. They seemed nice enough but didn't talk to Lisi much. Lunch was served, and after a filling meal Mrs. Hertz shooed everyone to the living room so she could finish pressing Jerry's clothes and start washing the new load he brought her.

Lisi stayed to help her mama. Every week was the same. New laundry arrived from soldiers in the barracks, and clean, pressed laundry would be sent back with Jerry.

The afternoon flew by and before Lisi knew it, Jerry stood and stretched. This week he invited her papa to join them in a soccer game. Mr. Hertz used to be a very good soccer player in Bamberg where he grew up. Lisi remembered he once told the story about how he brought the game to their small town when he moved there before he was married. The first day of playing, however, the police arrested him for indecent exposure because all the players wore shorts. "The town was filled with a bunch of old hens," he had said. Then the first war came and he hadn't played since. Now that he worked for the Americans, they often talked about soccer since a nice large field sat just on the other side of the fence that surrounded the barracks.

"Just one game, Otto? I wanna see these moves you boast about," Jerry teased. She was afraid how her papa would handle his jesting. To her surprise, he smiled.

"All right, one game. Then I have to get home to bed so I can be rested for work tomorrow." He stood, indicating it was time to leave.

Lisi knew he never went to bed early whether it was a work night or not, but she didn't say anything. She didn't want to bring on his wrath when he seemed to be in such a good mood. "Can we come watch, Papa?" Rille begged as she smiled at Jerry, who didn't even notice.

"Will you come too, Lea?" Jerry's eyes were somewhere else and it made Rille mad.

"Lea, have you received a letter lately from Johann?" Lisi secretly cheered when Rille asked about her husband.

Lea smiled at Jerry and explained that he still hadn't returned home yet. "Are you sure it's all right for us to go? I noticed the sign posted on the barbed wire the other day, forbidding German entry."

Jerry shifted uncomfortably. "That's just for the barracks themselves. The field is out back."

Lea turned to her papa. "Papa, can we all go?"

"Fine. Let's go." Everyone, even Mrs. Hertz, headed out, excited to watch a friendly game of American soccer with one German player.

CHAPTER 30

That night Lisi sat staring out the living room window, sulking. After the soccer game ended, the soldiers requested for Lea and Rille to stay and grab dinner. Permission granted from the officer, Jerry drove Lisi and her parents home while her sisters remained behind. Jerry promised to take care of them and drive them home after they ate.

Now Lisi waited, deeply sighing once more in exasperation. Why was she always the one being left behind? A small part of her wished her sisters would go back to Wurzburg, even though she knew they had said it would still be a long time until the city was restored. Not even the small farewell kiss on her cheek from Jerry helped to relieve her frustration. She was just about to check the time for the tenth time when she heard a car pull up.

Jumping up from her seat she ran to the door, but her mama stopped her short. Her papa had gone out, again. He left as soon as Jerry dropped them off. The sisters walked in talking and laughing. Jealousy ran through Lisi's veins.

"Hi, Mama. Hi, Little One." They gave a quick recap of the fun but uneventful evening, before heading to bed. Lisi trailed behind asking in vain for details.

As the girls all settled into their beds, car doors slammed and loud voices carried up through the window. Lisi looked over at her sisters' bed and jumped up for the window. "It's two soldiers. I've never seen them before."

"What?" Lea jumped out of her bed. "You must be mistaken. Let me see." She ran to the window and gasped. "Rille, it is the soldiers, and I don't think they're in their right minds tonight."

"What should we do?" Rille panicked.

"We need to hide. But where?"

Mrs. Hertz appeared in the bedroom doorway. "Girls, please stay up here. Two soldiers just pulled up and it's a little late for a social visit."

Lea and Rille gaped at each other, and for the first time Lisi realized there was more to the story of the night than they shared. Lea begged, "Mama, please do whatever it takes to make them leave. They must not find us. Please!"

Mrs. Hertz also made the connection. The knock came loud and hard. She nodded silently and pointed to the ceiling. Slowly she left the room, closed the door, and walked downstairs, slow and steady.

"Come on, Rille. The roof." Watching out the front window until the soldiers stepped inside, Lea silently slid the window open and climbed onto the front porch roof. Rille, shaking, followed.

Once they were safely outside, Rille turned back to Lisi. "Close the window and climb into bed. Don't say a word." Lisi nodded and quickly complied.

Only a second or two after she climbed into bed she heard her mama's loud voice. "I assure you, gentlemen, I haven't seen my daughters since we left them with you."

The bedroom door flew open and through squinted eyes Lisi saw two soldiers loom over her. "Well, well, well, what do we have here? You must be the 'little one.' Jerry's told us so much about you." One of the soldiers ripped the thin blankets from her body and she reactively pulled her legs up to her chest. Lisi didn't understand what they said, but she recognized Jerry's name. Had he talked to these dogs about her? She couldn't answer but just stared at the pin-shaped nose of the soldier who spoke to her. The other one she saw out of the corner of her eye rustled the blankets of her sisters' bed and searched the room.

"Where are your sisters? They told us they had to come right home to make their curfew, and now they aren't here. Where are they?" Lisi only stared at the red face as it twisted into a monster, and she held her breath while he breathed slurred words at her. She prayed her dinner didn't come back up.

"What, you got nothin' to say? I bet if Jerry was here you'd have a lot to say." He reached his hand to her and she shrank back, but the other soldier interrupted him.

"Come on, Hank. She's only a child. I bet those girls stopped off somewhere. Let's go find 'em." He slurred his words too, but at least he didn't seem angry like Hank.

Hank paused a minute longer, staring Lisi down before relenting. He tossed her blankets on the floor and left the room without another word.

Lisi didn't move until she heard the door close. All she wanted to do was curl up in a ball. Instead she ran to the window and raised it for her sisters.

Mrs. Hertz entered the room as Lea closed the window. All four Hertz girls hugged each other in one big hug. Mrs. Hertz never asked what really happened that night. Neither did Lisi. She remembered Fritz's advice. Sometimes the less you know, the better, and this was definitely one of those times.

CHAPTER 31

Jerry's usual knock came at the door the next morning. Lisi and her sisters sat finishing their breakfast. Mrs. Hertz hung laundry outside. Lisi's stomach twisted at the remembrance of what happened the previous night. Somehow, she blamed Jerry even though it wasn't his fault. Maybe because he was an American just like those monsters. Maybe all Americans were the same.

Usually she ran to answer the door, but this morning she let her papa get it. She didn't move as the door opened and her papa greeted Jerry. She waited for the door to close and the men to leave. Instead, she heard his voice. "Mr. Hertz, are Mama Hertz and Lea and Rille here?" Great. He had come inside.

Lea and Rille remained stoic as Jerry entered the kitchen. "Good morning." Lisi didn't reply. Her sisters did. They were always the nicer ones. "I just wanted to say how sorry I am for the conduct of my fellow American soldiers last night. They were completely out of line and I'm sorry. I'm so sorry." Geez, could he say he was sorry anymore? It didn't change what happened.

"Thank you," Rille replied. Lea managed a smile.

"No need for you to apologize, Son. I'm sure whatever it was, it wasn't as bad as all that. Come on, let's go."

Lisi did all she could to stay silent. After all it wasn't her situation and she would only be scolded for sticking her nose where it didn't belong. Before he left, Jerry touched the top of her head. "Hey, Little One."

She replied, "hey," but didn't look at him.

Jerry took the hint and didn't press her. "Good day."

It took several days for the Hertz girls to recover from what happened that night. Every time they walked down the street and passed an American soldier they wondered if he was nice, like Jerry, or awful, like Hank and Stephen. Most of the time the soldiers kept to themselves as they patrolled the streets, but once in a while one would sneer or call out, "Nazi."

One afternoon, Lisi, Rose, and Ruth were on their way home from swimming in the town pool when two soldiers promenaded toward them. The girls had come up with a system, a way of knowing if it was all right to look at soldiers and say hello or lower their eyes and walk by.

The nice ones had a certain walk and wore a kind expression. Today Ruth made the first observation. "Look down. Whatever you do, don't look at them."

The girls almost made it past but then one of the soldiers stepped out in front as the other one quickly followed, blocking their way. "Well, well, well, what do we have here? Little Nazis? Hello there. Where's your mama?"

Lisi recognized one of the soldiers immediately. She would remember the one called Hank anywhere. The girls linked arms and tried to avoid them, but the other soldier side-stepped to block them. Lisi looked to the ground and hid her face. "What's the matter, cat got your tongue?"

The girls didn't know what the soldiers said but it didn't sound nice. Rose replied in German, "Please let us by. We are late and our mamas will be worried."

The soldiers laughed at them. "Don't you know this is American territory now? Speak English."

After a long, intimidating minute, the soldiers, who weren't any older than Albert, grew tired and stepped aside. They laughed as the girls hurried by.

"Ruth, how did you know so quickly?" Rose asked.

Ruth wiped the beads of sweat from her lip. "I've seen that look before."

Lisi shivered even though the hot July sun beat down upon her.

For a while Lisi begrudged Jerry for what happened to her sisters. After that night he kept his distance, other than when it was his duty to pick up her papa. The girls heaved a sigh of relief after two weeks when Jerry had pick-up duty and he informed them a report had been filed against Hank and Stephen. They had already been transferred to a different unit.

Slowly things settled down and Jerry was welcomed once again as part of the Hertz family. Lea's husband returned the third week of July and the couple decided to return to Wurzburg, bringing Rille with them.

Many of the refugees chose to stay in town after the war while others moved on to find a new home in American-occupied territory. Ruth and her family were able to permanently settle in the small house near Lisi. None of their Jewish neighbors returned.

Mr. Hertz continued to work for the Americans at their barracks and helped Father Alder in his free time. Lisi stopped wondering about her papa's secret activity with Father Alder, or where he went during his extended times away from home. Her mama still prayed often but seemed more at peace since the end of the war. Lisi could tell she longed for the day when she would be reunited with her sons again. Everyone hoped that day came sooner than later. Overall life had definitely calmed down for Lisi and her family. Until August.

CHAPTER 32

August 2, 1945

"Mm, I fhink fhese are de beft booberries eber!" Lisi laughed as she held her hand up to her mouth to catch the flying blueberry pieces before they splattered all over Rose's face.

"What? I can't understand you with your face stuffed with blueberries." Rose joined in the fun by grabbing a few blueberries from her basket and hurling them at Lisi's face. Lisi ducked just in time and plucked the last few remaining berries of the season off the bush and stuffed them into her already full mouth. "I promised Mama I'd be able to find enough berries to bring home for one more pie." Looking into her half-full basket, Rose groaned. "I'd better keep looking. This isn't even close. I'm going over to the other side."

By now Lisi had swallowed and checked her own sparse pile of blueberries. "Not me. I'm here to eat. I didn't even tell Mama I was coming. She was too busy talking to Mrs. Berger. Come on. Let's go over there. The blueberries look bigger."

"I'm good right here. It's too bad Ruth couldn't come today. She would've at least helped me fill my basket, since you're so preoccupied. It's getting late. We should finish and start back down. Besides, Mama said to make sure we don't wander too close to the border."

Lisi was glad the friendship between Rose and Ruth continued to grow, but she rolled her eyes and regretted her suggestion. "We are not even close to the Soviet line. Come on, you wimp!" She danced in circles humming a song, purposely ignoring whatever argument Rose crafted. Only it wasn't Rose she heard. From somewhere nearby shouts filled the air. Sticks snapped and leaves crackled. The noise was growing louder.

Forgetting about the argument, Lisi and Rose ran toward each other. Grabbing Rose's arm, Lisi pulled her friend away from the noise. They were almost to the clearing when a soldier jumped out in front and pointed a gun directly at the girls. They both screamed as blueberries scattered to the ground. The girls turned to run back the way they came. "Stop! Don't move or I will shoot." By now Lisi had gotten pretty good at understanding English and this language was definitely not English. Neither understood what was said, but they thought it wasn't good to try to outrun a Russian soldier with a gun.

Frozen in place, the girls slowly raised their hands, nearly empty baskets dangled from their arms. "Turn around and start walking." Lisi caught a good look at the soldier and noticed he couldn't have been any older than Albert. Both girls stood, motionless with arms raised, staring at the young man. They knew he just gave them another order, but how were they supposed to follow it if they couldn't understand him?

Lisi found her voice and boldly replied. "The war is over. Germany is finished fighting. Why...."

"Turn around. Walk." There it was again, that strange language, only this time he gestured with his gun. She wasn't about to question him even though she had no idea what they did wrong. She also couldn't help but wonder how someone so young could be in such a position. Then she realized her brothers fought in the army for Hitler. Is this how they had become too? The war changed her parents, and it had definitely changed her. Why wouldn't it change her brothers too? This last thought depressed her so much that she hadn't even realized they were walking straight toward a barbed wire fence that cut through the field in both directions as far as Lisi could see.

Confusion mingled with fear spread across her face. She'd picked blueberries here every summer for as long as she could remember and she never remembered this fence. She turned her head slightly to try to capture Rose's expression, but something jabbed her in the back. Her head snapped to the center.

"This way!" The soldier pushed the girls harder. Why couldn't he comprehend they had no idea what he said? As they walked, he yelled to them again but this time he waved his arm madly to the left. An opening in the fence came into view as the trio mounted a small hill.

Dread filled Lisi as they approached the opening. The soldier pushed her through first with Rose on her heels. Lisi looked around as best she could for a way to escape, but to no avail. There was no place to hide even if they could get loose and run. And the gun. She had no doubt the soldier would use it on them.

They continued to walk for only a few minutes more before a brown building came into focus. Lisi didn't recognize it, but that sense of dread engulfed her. She wondered how Rose felt next to her.

"Lisi?" Rose's whispered plea answered her thought. She was terrified. Rose was always the cautious, sensible one who kept the daring Lisi out of trouble. As scared as Lisi felt, this must be a hundred times worse for Rose.

Afraid of making the soldier angrier, Lisi slowly inched closer to her friend and discreetly reached out to grab her hand. She squeezed it. The question that laid unanswered and untouched, like the blueberries sitting in their baskets, was would it really be all right?

CHAPTER 33

Two guards stood outside the building wielding guns like the other soldier. They yanked the baskets out of the girls' hands before shoving them through the doorway. Inside, it took a minute to adjust to the dim lighting. The odor that wafted into Lisi's nostrils produced the immediate automatic reaction to cover her nose and mouth with the palm of her hand so she wouldn't wretch. Rose let out a small cry and quickly covered her face too.

"Move." Again, the girls were forced forward. They practically marched down a long aisle past small rooms on both sides with bars for doors. Lisi gasped. This was some sort of jail. At least the cells were empty. In fact, the entire building stood empty except for the two guards and now another soldier who stood with the young one. The new soldier seemed to be about her papa's age, with graying hair at his temples, standing about six feet tall. Behind the hardness, his eyes seemed to have a tenderness, almost friendliness, behind the hardness of the lines around them.

After a brief conversation between the two men, the young soldier saluted and left the building. Turning to the girls the officer extended his hand and motioned for them to sit down. He positioned himself in the chair behind a desk, folded his hands on top, and asked in perfect German, "What were you doing in the woods?"

Startled by the fact that this man spoke their language, the girls looked at each other. Lisi read the question in Rose's eyes, *do we trust him?* What harm could come from answering honestly even if he did speak with a heavy accent? Lisi remembered her mama's words, "And you will know the truth, and the truth will set you free." She knew her mama recited this from somewhere in the Bible, but the thought of her mama right now overshadowed the fear with the same bravery she possessed when the refugees came.

"If we trust in Him, He will deliver us from evil." Was her mama there with her? Before she spoke she took a deep breath. "We were picking blueberries." The deep breath didn't help. Her voice still sounded shaky and weak. Then she added, "Sir." Lisi heard the laughter of the guards outside and wondered if they were reaping the benefits of the girls' hard work, enjoying the last pick of the season. Lisi could picture the laughter and ridicule as the guards popped berries into their slanderous mouths.

"You were picking blueberries? Are you sure that's all you were doing?"

"Yes, Sir," Lisi responded and Rose nodded beside her.

The man was quiet, and Lisi lifted her eyes as far as they would go without raising her head. She remembered years ago when a neighbor had spoken to her and, afraid of him, she looked at the ground to answer. Her papa grabbed her arm and squeezed so tightly that she automatically lifted her head. With angry eyes he silently spoke to her soul, commanding her to make eye contact with the neighbor. He kept his hold on her arm until she looked at him.

Sitting in the dark, damp hallway, Lisi rubbed her arm as if her papa was there, squeezing it again. She knew she should look at the officer, but she couldn't bring herself to lift her head. She didn't know why. What did she have to hide, other than the fear in her eyes that might reveal her lack of bravery?

"Where are these blueberries?" The loud voice echoed through the girls' ears, and Lisi suddenly saw the salt and pepper stubble on the man's face in front of her. In the same instant he moved to Rose, asking her the same question.

An otherworldly strength shot through Lisi, and bravery filled the places where her fear coursed a minute ago. It took her by surprise, but she knew what she needed to do. She had to protect her friend. They hadn't done anything wrong. While the officer's eyes may have seemed kind, she didn't know what he was capable of doing, and she didn't want to find out.

Lifting her weary head she looked directly at him and answered for Rose. "The blueberries you are looking for have been stolen from us by your soldiers and eaten." She didn't know if this last part was true, but what harm would come from adding it?

To both girls' surprise and astonishment, the officer stood up and tilted his head back as a small chuckle turned into a deep, roaring laugh. One of the guards rushed in. "Sir, is everything all right?" In reply the officer could only nod and speak a single word which the girls assumed meant 'yes,' even though they didn't know for sure what the solider asked.

Finally calming down, the officer called the two guards in and ordered them to lead the girls to a cell. Lisi's guard pulled open the gate and shoved her inside. The second guard did the same to Rose. Slamming the door closed, one guard locked it and smiled at the girls through the bars. His smile sent shivers down Lisi's spine, and she was grateful when both men left. The officer approached them, spoke in his language, and followed the guards outside.

"Are you all right?" Lisi rushed to Rose and pulled her into a tight hug as soon as the door to the building shut. Rose began to cry, and Lisi finally let her own tears come as the girls held on to each other, unsure of what the next hours would bring.

CHAPTER 34

Unable to sleep, Lisi rested on the small, hard slab, thinking about everything that happened. After the girls calmed down, they spent hours trying to figure out how they came to be here, arrested, locked in prison somewhere in an unknown location. They neglected to answer the one question that blared at them. Why? It clearly seemed nobody believed their story of blueberry picking. Who did the officer think they were? He made it perfectly clear he trusted the girls about as much as he trusted the blueberries they picked.

Lisi thought about her family. Her mama must be beside herself with worry. She doubted that her papa would even notice her absence. She pictured her mama, standing at the same window she used to stand at when they listened to the forbidden radio programs during the war. Her mama was so strong, so bold and so brave. Talking to a refugee girl was one thing, but this took on a whole new form of bravery. Lisi hoped she would be half as brave as her mama.

In the middle of this thought a realization struck her. She was like her mama! She stood up to the officer and addressed his questions with an unexplained boldness. She thought for a while, wondering where the strength came from. Not one tear fell, and through her singing she had been able to comfort Rose.

There, locked in a foreign jail, Lisi felt overwhelmed by a renewed strength. Again, she marveled. *I am like Mama.* This unexplained strength, she remembered her mama said, came from Jesus.

A deep longing overtook her. *Now if I could only have the same peace that Mama has.* Realizing how similar they were, Lisi wanted more. She wanted to be able to stand up to anybody who came against her and bravely declare what she believed in just like her mama did that day in their foyer with Mr. Richter. The problem was, Lisi didn't know how to do it.

She decided right there in that jail cell to do what she knew how to do. She prayed, asking God to help her to be brave, for herself as well as for Rose. The rising sun cast shadows through the tiny window of the cell. *How can Rose sleep right now?* She thought it was better to let her be since neither of them had any idea of what would happen next.

A door slammed followed by a loud bang. "Lisi?" Rose was awake now.

"It's all right, Rose. I'm here. Take my hand. God will help us." Loud, heavy boots approached the one occupied cell. The old officer who interrogated the girls yesterday stood in front of them. "Well, young ladies, we have determined that you are not spies. You are being released." He unlocked the door and held it open.

Without saying a word, the girls jumped to their feet and flew out of the cell. Lisi stopped for a moment once she was out of the officer's reach and turned around. "You thought we were spies? Why?" Rose did not care to hear his response and yanked her friend out the door.

By now the blaring sun shone its rays down so brightly that the two girls had to stop and blink a few times before they could see anything. Once they adjusted to the light they stepped off the platform nearly tripping over two buckets. A snicker from behind caused them to turn around. Two guards stood on either side of the doorway. They both smiled. The one who snickered said something to them in Russian, making both guards burst out laughing. The girls turned back to the buckets to find their precious blueberries. Quickly they grabbed their buckets and raced all the way home, losing only a few berries along the way.

CHAPTER 35

Fall 1945

Foreign words stared up at Lisi as the English book Jerry gave her sat open in her lap. It was a cool autumn afternoon. Her papa should be on his way home from his job at the base, and her mama sliced bread, getting ready for dinner. Lisi had no homework and no other distractions. It was really a perfect time to study her English. It didn't matter that she believed English to be the most difficult language to learn. It was part of their promise. Jerry made her promise to try to learn English if he promised to continue his study of German, right after he made her promise the next time she left town to go berry picking, she'd tell him so he could accompany her. Lisi understood and agreed, remembering how relieved everyone felt after she and Rose had been released from the Soviet prison. However, she also added an amendment. Jerry must bring her bubble gum whenever he had some and he was required to teach her all the latest songs and dances, like the jitterbug. She hoped he would give her some more chewing gum for her thirteenth birthday in a couple of weeks.

She laid the book down and walked to her window, singing a new song Jerry taught her by someone named Perry, even though that wasn't his real name. She smiled as she noticed him walking down the road. It looked like he was headed for her house. As he came closer, she could see his face more clearly. He didn't look happy. Why didn't he drive the truck? "No, Jerry, don't tell us you're being transferred," she spoke to the window. She heard his familiar knock and practiced her jitterbug moves out her door and down the stairs. Maybe if she showed him she still hadn't mastered the dance, he would stay.

"Hey, Little One." The way he said her nickname with his American accent in broken German wasn't even enough to make her smile today as she looked at his face.

"What's wrong, Shori?" *Don't tell me you're leaving.*

Giving her a slight grin, Jerry answered. "Is your mama home?"

The last six months of getting to know him had prepared Lisi enough to know something happened. She had a feeling it was even worse than what she originally thought. She pointed to the kitchen. "She's in there preparing dinner. Is everything all right?"

Jerry nodded and followed Lisi into the kitchen. "Mama, Shori is here. He wants you."

He greeted Mrs. Hertz, "Hello, Mama. Please forgive me for barging in like this, but there's been an accident. The jeep ran off the road. Otto and two of our soldiers were badly hurt. They've been transported to the hospital in Wurzburg. The police are investigating to see if there might be a connection with the Nuremberg Trials that have just ended."

"An accident?" Thoughts swirled through Lisi's mind as she processed what Jerry said. Papa had been hurt. Lisi didn't want to care. She hated her papa. She knew she shouldn't think that, but she couldn't help it. She had been glad that he hadn't been around much lately because when he wasn't around he couldn't hurt her or her mama. But now he was the one hurt, and Lisi knew she should be more concerned. She remembered again what her mama said about praying to God for help. Hadn't God helped her out of the Soviet prison? This was different, though. How could she pray for her papa when each day she disliked him even more? Before she could reason her way out of it, Lisi mumbled a short prayer for her papa, even if she didn't wholeheartedly mean it.

She figured she must've been invisible just then because neither Jerry nor her mama even flinched when she spoke. "Related to the Trials?" Her mama processed this new information.

Lisi had heard of the Nuremberg Trials from the radio. They took place in Nuremberg, Germany, and were trials for twenty-two of the worst Nazi criminals. Lisi figured it had to be important because the radio announcer talked about the four judges, one from four different countries. None of those countries was Germany, however. The judges came from the Allied countries: Great Britain, the United States, France, and the Soviet Union. Lisi wondered what Jerry thought these trials had to do with her papa's accident.

He had responded to her mama's question but Lisi missed it, too busy in her own thoughts. Jerry finished and the silence seemed louder than her mama's heavy breathing. Mrs. Hertz held one hand over her mouth while she gripped the counter with the other. Lisi wondered whether her mama really cared about her papa or if it was an act.

"And one more thing." *Just spit it out,* Lisi brooded. Why did he have to be so dramatic?

"Go ahead, Jerry. Whatever it is, I want to know." Mrs. Hertz took a deep, shaky breath.

"They think it was intentional." Jerry danced around the truth, Lisi just knew. Her mama didn't push him for details, so she held her tongue.

Shortly after, Jerry hugged Mrs. Hertz and waved to Lisi before parting. She stared at him. He had changed so much in the last six months. He was more handsome than before. His tanned face and bright blue eyes seemed even darker and brighter. Maybe it wasn't his looks as much as his personality, the way he smiled and made himself feel at home every time he came over that changed. Lisi knew it wouldn't last forever, and because of that she was both grateful and sad.

Part of her hoped her papa would recover, maybe just not right away. Here came the guilty feelings again. In some ways it was better this way. Now she could be there to support her mama. Maybe her papa would forget everything he had done in the past, like some sort of amnesia. That would be good. Then they could bridge the ravine that stretched for miles between them.

An accident. The words danced around in Lisi's mind again as she followed her mother through the hospital doors in Wurzburg. The wing of the hospital that housed her papa remained mostly intact. The rubble from the damaged wing was a dark reminder of how much remained of the destruction.

Her stomach flip flopped. She tried to calm her nerves by humming quietly, but even that didn't help. What would she say to him? She rarely saw him now. She didn't even know him, and he didn't know her anymore either.

Her mama sensed her uneasiness, and she reached her open hand behind her. The familiar warmth felt good. She couldn't believe how calm her mama acted. Lisi knew her papa emotionally detached from her mama years ago, and yet she acted as if she was about to walk into the room to see the only man she loved. Maybe she really did still love him? Lisi thought about Peter. Did she love Peter or did the emotions that she hid so deeply fill a void from the absence of her brothers? They were good friends, Peter like a brother to her. It made sense that she would love him like a brother.

After receiving the information at the desk, Mrs. Hertz led Lisi down the usable hallway and soon they entered a large room. Lisi looked around. Rows of beds filled the entire room. Most of the beds held wounded soldiers. Six months after the war ended and still so many. Lisi wondered if her brothers laid in any of the beds. She knew they didn't because her mama would have been notified. Still, they were somebody's brothers, somewhere. That made Lisi feel even more sad, wishing she stood here to visit her brothers instead of her papa.

His bed sat in a back corner of the room. A large bandage wrapped around his head like a mummy, his face, almost unrecognizable. Her eyes rested on a bandage that protected his shoulder. Under the blankets, she couldn't see the other injuries. For the first time Lisi wondered what happened to him. He looked like a corpse. He must have sensed their presence because he slowly opened his eyes. Lisi stood in his view.

Moaning, he tried to focus his attention on her but almost instantly closed his eyes again and wrinkled his eyebrows. Lisi wanted to say something to him but she didn't know what, so she just stood there quietly. She looked at her mama across the bed and relaxed a little. Her mama looked so calm and peaceful as she quietly spoke to her papa. She couldn't hear what she said because she spoke in a soft voice, close to his ear. At one point she closed her eyes, and Lisi knew she was praying. How strange that her mama would do that after the way he treated them. It made Lisi sad to see the love her mama still had for him. She prayed that God would ease her mama's pain.

An older nurse came in then, practically shoving them out the door. "He needs his rest," she kept repeating. As soon as Lisi and her mama were out of the way, the crotchety old nurse spoke. "Gretel, help me change the dressing on this gunshot wound."

Gunshot wound? "Wait here, Little One. I'll be right back." Mrs. Hertz's body stiffened as she approached her papa's bed again. "Excuse me, but did I overhear you correctly? Does my husband have a gunshot wound?"

The nurse called Gretel looked up from her work. "Just a small one. Not to worry, dear. It will heal nicely." Two words came to Lisi's mind. Nuremberg Trials.

CHAPTER 36

A month later Mr. Hertz had been released from the hospital but transferred to a mental facility. Lisi didn't understand everything, but she knew his vocal chords had somehow been damaged in the accident. He couldn't really speak yet. She also knew the rest of his body was expected to recover, including the gunshot wound, but something happened to his brain and the doctors weren't sure what his mental capacity would be.

Her mama asked her on several occasions if she wanted to go visit him, making it clear how often her sisters did. Each time she refused. She wasn't sure she wanted to go to a place like that. However, one Saturday in mid-November something happened that compelled her to see him.

She worked at the church all day like usual, welcoming the stragglers of new refugees and feeding those who stayed at the parish. She was tired and just finished her last duty for the day. As she walked by a group of newcomers to get her coat, someone grabbed her leg. She tripped and would have fallen, but she reached out and balanced herself on the wall.

Lisi looked at her captor and saw a man a little older than her papa, wrapped tightly in a blanket. He looked like he had lost a hundred pounds, and his facial hair suggested he had been traveling for a long time. But she noticed something else too. This man did not look like the others. He sat with a group of German refugees who traveled from Poland but didn't seem like he belonged. "Excuse me, Fräulein Hertz?" He whispered perfect German. She froze and her blood ran cold.

"What do you want?" Lisi wiped the palm of her hands on her skirt. "Who are you?"

"Forgive me, but that is not important. I wonder if you would be willing to give your papa a message for me. Your papa is Otto Hertz, no?" Lisi stared. He smiled a crooked smile. "Tell him it's from an old friend. Tell him we must all pay for our sins. Lha-cha-eh...tkin...dzeh." Exhausted, the old man leaned back against the wall.

Frightened, Lisi turned to leave as quickly as she could. She sensed something awful lay in the meaning of what the strange man said, and she needed to get away from him.

"Fräulein Hertz?" *Oh, what did he want now?* She stopped but didn't turn around. Who was this man? Did she want to know how he knew her papa? Once again Fritz's caution entered her mind, so as curious as she was, she didn't want to know anything. After all, did it really matter?

"Tell him Von Gross sends his greetings, and I apologize we didn't have a chance to catch up when we saw each other last — one month ago."

One month ago? Did he? Was he? Lisi couldn't finish a thought. She ran away as fast as her legs could carry her.

Leaving the church, Lisi let the autumn wind blow across her face as she contemplated what to do next. Should she tell her mama and add to her worries? Should she tell her papa and risk possibly hindering his recovery? Maybe she should talk to Rose, whose papa had been home for a month and might know more about what the man was talking about? Or Ruth, who, being a refugee herself, might know him personally? Lisi knew the latter idea was far-fetched since Ruth and her family came more than six months ago, but she decided it might be the best place to start. Maybe she would be able to explain what his chilling words meant.

By the time Lisi knocked on Ruth's door, she knew what she really needed to do. She needed to talk to her papa. Only he would be able to solve the mystery. Since she already knocked, she waited for an answer. Footsteps approached on the other side.

"Oh, hello, Lisi."

"Hello, Peter." Why did he have to answer the door? And why did he only see her as another sister? Lisi couldn't let him distract her right now. She had a mission to complete. "Is Ruth home?"

Peter shook his head. "I'm sorry, she's at the store with Mama right now. Did you need something? Are you all right?"

She didn't realize how heavily she was breathing until she saw his odd expression. Nodding, she thanked him before leaving. Was she out of breath from running to their house, or from seeing him standing in the doorway? It didn't matter. She had no excuse now to procrastinate the inevitable. She knew her mama would take her in a heartbeat. Like it or not, it was time for answers. It was time to visit her papa.

CHAPTER 37

"Little One."

Lisi's body prickled. Coming out of his mouth, the hoarse, whispered nickname sounded almost sickening to her ears. At the same time, though, a longing stirred deep inside. She tried to smile. "Hi, Papa. The doctors said you're going to be just fine, now that you've started to talk again."

Her papa closed his eyes, and Lisi could tell he was trying to ignore the pain and find the strength to tell her something. He shook his head. She looked at her mama who stood across from her. She nodded. Lisi looked back to her papa and waited.

"Sometimes...life...things happen...." Lisi knew where this was going. She didn't want to hear it. She didn't care. Anger began to rise up inside her, but when he opened his eyes again and looked at her, she saw something she didn't expect to see. She saw regret. And pain.

"I shouldn't...shouldn't have...Nazis...too much...." With each word she watched her papa struggle more and more. Tears silently fell down her mama's face. Did she know something? Had God answered her mama's prayers and brought her papa back to Him?

A single tear escaped his eye and ran down his bruised cheek. *He does have feelings,* Lisi thought to herself as she watched him struggle to speak.

"I'm...sorry...." Then he stopped. He closed his eyes again and turned his head back to the center. Lisi watched his chest, waiting for it to rise again. It didn't. Her papa was gone, and this time for good.

The nurse on duty popped her head in the doorway. "Time's up, folks. Otto needs his rest. You can come back tomorrow." Lisi knew there would be no tomorrow. She and her mama stood rooted in place as they stared at her papa. Exasperated, the nurse started to repeat herself then stopped mid-sentence.

She pushed past Mrs. Hertz and checked his vitals. Feeling nothing, she ran into the hallway and quickly returned with a man in a white coat. Lisi figured he must be the doctor. What happened next blurred together. Someone pushed Lisi out of the way to the corner of the room, people jostled in and out, some talked to each other, and some talked to her mama, who stood dumbfounded staring at them as if they spoke a different language. The only memory Lisi had of that afternoon was that she didn't cry one tear as she watched her papa lay in front of her, dead.

An hour later Lisi and her mama bounced about on a northbound train headed home. She hadn't said a word as she struggled with what she should be feeling and what she actually felt. Her mama didn't even seem to notice.

Two things fought for control of Lisi's mind, but she had the strange sense they were connected. She knew if she didn't ask her mama about it now, the courage might leave her forever. She couldn't stop thinking about that last conversation with her papa and how she never had the chance to ask him her question. The entire purpose of the trip and her mission failed. She took a deep breath. "Mama?"

Mrs. Hertz turned from the window, revealing fresh tears that flowed freely down her face. Lisi leaned into her and welcomed the arm that wrapped around her shoulders. How could she ask her mama now? It would only make her more upset. Maybe she could ask one of her brothers when they came home. If they came home. Oh, but this was the perfect opportunity now. Just the two of them and an hour with no distractions. How long would it be before she had another chance? Or maybe there would be too many opportunities, now that it would be just the two of them at home until the boys returned. "What is it, Little One?"

How different her nickname sounded coming out of her mama's mouth. The struggle between concern for her mama and overwhelming curiosity raged within her. Not to mention the nagging feeling in the back of Lisi's soul that kept reminding her she should be grieving for her papa.

Forget those thoughts now. Lisi could punish herself later. Right now, she needed to ask her mama or she would burst. "Um, Papa...." She couldn't do it. "Nothing, Mama."

The rest of the trip passed in silence. At home Lisi locked herself in her room for the rest of the night. Her mama had sent a message to Lea and Rille, and they arrived at the house shortly after Lisi and Mrs. Hertz.

Lisi heard them come in but didn't care. She listened to her mama explain how worried she was about her. She hadn't meant to worry her mama.

"Lisi?" Her mama opened the door and laid on the bed next to her, patiently waiting. Lisi felt badly, as she lay there completely still. She usually told her mama everything, but now she just couldn't. Her mama would think she was the worst person in the entire world. She wasn't even talking to God right now.

Next Rille came in and tried to talk. Even though Lisi thought she was too bossy, the girls had a special bond.

Rille didn't knock. She let herself in and perched herself on the edge of her own bed. Her tears fell softly down her round cheeks. "Little One, we are all grieving for Papa. It's all right. It's normal. Come downstairs with us so we can all be together." Lisi buried her face even deeper in her arms on her pillow. If Rille only knew why Lisi really cried she wouldn't be asking for her company.

Finally, after a belaboring one-sided conversation between sobs, Rille gave up and left. A little while later Lea came in. Lisi always considered her the gentle one. At least she stood outside the door and knocked softly. "Lisi?" Lisi could tell she had been crying too. "Lisi, can I come in?"

What a dumb question. *It's your room too,* Lisi thought. Then she realized it had been at one time, but not anymore. It made Lisi feel respected when her sister asked permission, recognizing the changes that took place over time.

Lea knocked again. "Lisi, I'm coming in. You don't have to say anything. I just want to be with you. Mama's worried about you. So are we." The door creaked. Lisi felt her sister's presence, but she made no movements. After a minute Lea walked over and knelt down next to the bed. She gently stroked Lisi's hair.

For a while a heavy silence covered the room like a dark rain cloud. Lisi wished her sister would go away, but she had to admit, it felt good to have her here playing with her hair just like their mama used to do. Lisi pretended Lea knew what she really felt and loved her anyway. It was as if with each stroke of her hand she wiped away the guilt and shame that hovered over Lisi's head. It must have been the motherly instinct she used to have with her.

As her sister continued, Lisi wished she could open up. She also wished that if she did, Lea would keep it a secret and not tell their mama. Her mama couldn't find out. So Lisi stayed quiet, feeling the weight of everything release slowly.

"I have a secret that I haven't told anybody. But I want to tell you." Lisi stilled as she waited, her mind already playing with ideas.

"Remember the family I told you about? The one I worked for when I first moved to Wurzburg?"

Lisi waited, then nodded slightly. Was she finally going to hear all about the job and why Lea had lost the sparkle in her eyes?

"The Schneiders. Herr Schneider was a high-ranking official in Hitler's army." Lea paused. "Well, Herr Schneider wasn't a very nice man." Boy, what a revelation! Lisi had already figured out that pretty much anyone working for Hitler was not a nice person. "His wife was quite nice, but she wasn't home very often. Somehow Herr Schneider made sure he had business to take care of at home many times when the house was almost vacant, except for me." Lisi's stomach began to hurt like that day she saw Jerry come to her door after her papa's accident.

"Herr Schneider acted really nice to me from the beginning. Too nice. He didn't even talk to his wife as sweetly as he spoke to me. At first, I thought he wanted to make sure I was happy with my job. Until one day as I cleaned the living room he asked me to come into his office. He said he wanted to speak with me. I thought I was in trouble." Lea chuckled dryly at the memory.

"I stood in the doorway, uncomfortable at the thought of entering his private office. He called me over to his desk and stepped close to me. It made me very uncomfortable, and that was when I realized something wasn't right. But it was too late. He spoke words to me and then held my arms and kissed me hard. It hurt. I tried to pull away, but he wouldn't let me. After he let go, the gink threatened me if I told anyone. He also threatened me if I quit my job. Of course, I was too mortified to speak, so I excused myself and left as quickly as I could. Just as I stepped into the foyer, Frau Schneider returned home. I must have looked awful because she asked me if I felt all right. I told her I felt sick, so she released me for the rest of the day. I ran home to my apartment and cried. I was all alone. Johann was gone, I hadn't made many friends yet, and you were all here. I didn't know how I would be able to go back and face that man the next day. I also wondered if I had done something to make him think it was all right to treat me that way."

Lisi heard the pain in her sister's voice and slowly pulled herself up. How could she think it was her fault? Lea smiled at her, pushed her tear-soaked hair off her face, and tucked it behind her ears. So many questions filled Lisi's mind. "What happened the next day? Did you go to work? Did he ever do it again? And, uh, what's a gink?"

Lea smiled a sad smile. "Johann uses that word anytime he mentions a former member of the Nazi party. It means a stupid person."

"I could think of worse things to call that man than stupid."

Lea ignored the comment. "I did go to work the next day. I remembered what Mama used to tell me about being brave even when we're afraid. Frau Schneider was home, so of course Herr Schneider acted as if nothing ever happened. I was grateful for that, but only a couple of days later, we were alone again. When he called for me, I tried to make up excuses — too busy, had plans after work so I needed to finish quickly, and even that I was married. None of it mattered to him. It didn't matter to any of them. I was just another pretty face."

"I hate the Nazis!" Lisi never used to talk like that, yet recently it had become easier and easier to hate. "They're awful people. Maybe Papa was a Nazi?" Lisi slapped her hand over her mouth. She didn't mean to say that out loud. Would Lea be angry at her?

"No, Lisi. Don't say that. They weren't all like Herr Schneider. Believe it or not some of them were very nice. One officer even tried to help me before I quit. And remember, Johann also fought for the Germans. As did our brothers. And you remember what Papa always said about Hitler and the Nazi movement."

"Yeah, but they weren't real Nazis. They had no choice. Are you going to tell Mama?"

"I will tell Mama, now that it's over, but not right away. She has enough to worry about right now. But I wanted to tell you. I thought maybe if I shared a secret, you might want to share a secret with me?"

"I can't. It's nothing, really, but I think I'm ready to come downstairs." If her sister could share her deepest, darkest secret, the least Lisi could do was make her feel like it meant something. And it did. Lisi felt awful for what happened to her sister, but she also saw a change in her. A good change. Even though something bad happened, something good came out of it. "Lea, it wasn't your fault."

Lisi sat up on the bed and Lea pulled her sister into a hug. "I know," Lea whispered. She offered her hand to her youngest sister, and Lisi joined her small family downstairs. Even while she grieved on the outside with her family, however, her tears weren't for the reason they all believed.

CHAPTER 38

Lisi woke with a terrible headache. She opened her eyes but couldn't seem to make her body get out of bed. It was Sunday. Her mama never missed church, and that was the last place she wanted to be. She didn't want to see or talk to anybody, most of all God. What would He want her there for? She spent half the night tossing and turning, condemning herself. God didn't want her at church. He probably condemned her too.

Lisi begged to stay home, but of course her mama refused. She said they needed God more than ever right now. Lisi wondered about that. Even the thought of seeing Rose and Ruth didn't make her feel better.

She spent the entire service slouched in the pew between her mama and Lea. She avoided her friends' gazes and didn't sing the songs she loved. Not even when her mama elbowed her. After church she made an excuse to her mama about not feeling well and raced home. She knew she would have to explain to her friends, but not today. Rose always had a big family dinner on Sundays, and Ruth and her family always spent the day together too.

She climbed right into bed after ripping her church clothes off and tossing them on the floor. She'd get in trouble for that but she didn't care. There were more important things in life than wrinkled clothes. Her mama came up to check on her. Lisi told her she had a bad headache. It was true; she wasn't lying. Her mama reluctantly left, and she cried.

Fifteen minutes later a knock on the door startled her. She figured it was Lea, so she ignored it. The knock came again. And again. And again.

When it was clear Lisi wasn't going to be left in peace, she threw off her blankets and answered the door in attack mode. Immediately she stopped when her two best friends stood before her. "Rose. Ruth. I thought...I mean, I didn't know...what are you doing here?" She left the door open without waiting for an answer and climbed back onto her bed.

The two girls sat down on either side of Lisi. She hoped they would see her misery and leave her alone. Somehow, she doubted it. Ruth spoke first. Nope, they weren't going away. "I was hungry, and you gave me something to eat. I was thirsty, and you gave me something to drink. I was a stranger here, and you took me in."

Lisi recognized those words from the Bible when Jesus preached, but she didn't understand why Ruth recited it to her and how it explained their presence in her bedroom. "So?"

"You were the only one who helped me in my darkest hour. Now I'm here to help you in yours." Ruth put her arm around Lisi.

"We both are." From the other side Rose did the same.

"You don't understand. It's not what you think."

"How do you know what we think, Lisi? I will tell you what I think. I think your papa just died, and you are feeling badly because you don't feel as sad as you should. And because of that, you're reveling in self-pity, thinking you're an awful person who will go straight to hell because of it, and you are afraid to tell anybody because of what they will think of you." Ruth took a breath. "But most importantly, you are afraid of what God thinks of you. That is what I think."

Lisi stared at Ruth, her jaw dropped. How did she know? Should she admit it, or should she lie to keep the truth hidden?

Ruth smiled as if the silent reply confirmed she was correct. "Lisi, haven't you ever heard of King David?"

"Of course, I have. He was a great king. So?"

"Did you know the Bible says that God actually called David a man after His own heart? God never said that about anybody else in the whole Bible."

"So what?"

"So, what is one of the first things we think about when we think of King David?"

Realization began to dawn on Lisi. "He killed an innocent man so he could hide his affair with Bathsheba."

"Right. And who was Bathsheba?"

"The man's wife."

"Who else was she?"

"I don't know. A princess?"

Ruth shook her head. "Bathsheba was Jesus' twenty-five times great-grandma, making David his twenty-five times great-grandpa." She paused to let her point sink in. "Don't you see, Lisi? David had the wrong thoughts and feelings, and he acted on them. Then he had an innocent man murdered. And yet God knew how much David loved Him and wanted to have a heart for Him. So much that even after all his sins God gave David and Bathsheba a son whose lineage included Jesus Christ.

"Your papa hurt you and was mean to you for a long time. You have every right to be angry and hurt. God knows that you're hurting, and He wants to help you forgive yourself and be able to heal. But you have to first recognize that God still loves you no matter what, and He is the only one who can help you. Talk to Him, Lisi."

"What if He doesn't listen? I don't think He loves me anymore."

"Lisi, those are all lies. Remember the tapestry? The beautiful, safe, tapestry of lies Hitler created?"

Lisi nodded and glanced at Rose. They never talked about all that happened between them, but brushed it under a rug so that their differences remained hidden beneath a more important friendship. She hoped Rose didn't feel uncomfortable now, being here, because she was so glad she had come.

Thoughtfully, Rose just nodded and took Lisi's hand into hers, confirming that no matter what had happened, the bond they shared was stronger.

Ruth continued. "This is the same thing. These lies you think in your head are not from God, Lisi. He is love.

He forgives. If you seek Him with your heart, you will find Him."

It made sense. All of it. Lisi wanted to forgive her papa. After all, God forgave King David, and God could forgive her too.

Later that night, Lisi prayed a prayer to an unseen God that changed her life forever. She knew He was there, listening, because as a little girl she had prayed with her mama and asked Jesus into her heart. She needed Ruth's reminder that He was still there and still loved her no matter what.

When she finished, she pulled the covers over her head and cried. She cried long and hard, but this time it was different. It was a cleansing cry. She didn't cry because of her guilt or her shame. She cried for her papa. The sweet sense of relief overwhelmed Lisi. When no more tears would come, she took a deep breath and fell into a deep, peaceful sleep.

CHAPTER 39

Monday after school Lisi and Ruth decided to go to Rose's house while her mama and sisters made preparations. As the girls sat in Rose's living room, they chatted about school that day. After everything that happened over the weekend, Lisi completely forgot about the strange man in the church until now.

"I forgot to tell you both something." Lisi waited for silence, but her friends continued talking, something about soldiers coming home. Huffing, she cleared her throat and tried again. "It's about a refugee man I saw at church Saturday."

"Oh, yes, that's Alwin. Lisi used to think he was special."

Lisi couldn't believe her friends. "Did you hear me?" She stood up and practically shouted. "I met a man at the church. He was with the refugees, but I know he's not one of them. He knew my papa."

Finally. She had their attention. "How do you know?" Rose asked.

"Where did he say he was from? What was his name?" Ruth wondered, since she often went to the church looking for more family or friends she might know.

Lisi sat back, content to be the object of their attention. She looked at Rose. "I just know he's not one of them. I know it in here." She put her hands over her stomach. "And I don't know where he was from. I didn't ask him, but he told me to tell my papa that Von Gross sends his greetings. Whatever that means."

"Von Gross? Don't know him." Ruth shook her head and shrugged as if to indicate the conversation was over.

"But that's not all." Lisi leaned forward. Rose and Ruth followed, ready to hear what else she had to say. "He knew me. And like I already told you he said he knew my papa. He said he saw him a month ago, and he told me he had a message for him."

"What kind of message?" Ruth asked loudly, and the two girls quickly shushed her. They both knew that if Rose's mama heard about this she'd worry so much Rose wouldn't ever be able to leave the house again.

Lisi looked around to make sure they were really alone. Then she recalled the words from memory. "He said, 'tell him we must all pay for our sins,' and he apologized for not being able to catch up when they saw each other a month ago. A month ago." Lisi waited for it to sink in but her friends stared blankly at her. "My papa's accident happened a month ago. But that's not all. He said some odd phrase."

"Well, do you remember the phrase?" Rose was becoming impatient.

"Of course I do. What do you think, I'm stupid? He said, 'lha-cha-eh...tkin...dzeh.'" She repeated the phrase back just as he had said it to her. Even as she said it out loud shivers traveled down her spine like a xylophone, one vertebrae at a time.

"What?" both her friends said in unison. Lisi repeated the phrase, this time a little louder. Just as she finished a voice caused all three girls to jump.

"Lisi, where did you learn that?" Mr. Meyer stood, leaning against the doorway with his arms folded across his chest. He wore a very strange expression on his face. Lisi always liked him, but today she couldn't tell if he was angry, or sad, or scared. She looked at Rose, pleading for help.

"Papa. We didn't hear you come in. Lisi was just, uh, she was telling...." Rose had no idea how to finish her sentence without the risk of getting her friend in trouble.

Mr. Meyer walked slowly into the room and drew his armchair closer to the girls. Lisi noticed both arms had holes and stuffing poked out like curly white hair. *Just like Herr Von Gross,* she remembered. He slowly lowered himself until he sat comfortably, arms covering the holes. His expression never changed. "Now, Lisi. Can you please repeat those words again?"

Lisi knew it might get her into big trouble, but then again if it did, the man who called himself Von Gross shouldn't have said them in the first place. She began. "lha-cha-eh...tkin...," together, Mr. Meyer and Lisi repeated the last word, "dzeh."

He sat back in his chair and stroked his beard. Three sets of eyes stared at him, waiting. Finally, he spoke. "Lisi, where did you learn that?" His tone softened, and his face didn't look quite as scary as before. Lisi felt safe telling him.

"A man in the church. A refugee man. Well, he sat with the refugees but I know he really wasn't. At least not a refugee like the others. There was something different about him. I don't know, but he just seemed different. He called me by my name and told me to give that message to my papa. But when I went to tell my papa...." Her voice trailed off. She didn't need to finish. Everyone knew what she was going to say. Mr. Meyer stared at her frightened face as if choosing his next words very carefully. "Girls, sometimes what we see on the surface covers the reality of something deeper. In other words, what we think we see isn't always what is real. Do you understand?" The girls nodded in unison.

"Like a tapestry."

"That's exactly right, Lisi."

Lisi and Ruth exchanged a knowing glance, and Lisi thought about Albert. He had said the same thing to her a year ago when she saw him last.

"Those words are from a special code. Each word stands for a letter. Lha-cha-eh stands for the letter 'd.' tkin is the letter 'i.' And dzeh...." He paused before finishing. "Dzeh stands for the letter 'e.'"

The girls looked at him, confusion written all over their faces. "When you put those three letters together, in English they spell "die." Lisi gasped.

"Papa, how do you know that?" Rose asked the obvious question.

"During the war I belonged to an organization called the Resistance. It was a secret organization to overthrow Hitler and his army."

Lisi thought about Fritz and Albert. It surprised her Mr. Meyer had been part of it too. She looked at Rose who sat speechless and looked as if she could cry. It was obvious she had no idea. She wondered how Rose felt now about some of the beliefs and feelings she had felt toward Hitler. "Papa, I had no idea."

Mr. Meyer continued, "As part of the Resistance, I worked secretly with other soldiers in the German army as well as from America and France, mostly. The American Army developed a special code to transmit over the radios so the German army wouldn't know what they said. Those three words were part of the code."

The room was silent as the new information sunk in. Rose broke the silence. "Did you know who this Von Gross man was?"

Mr. Meyer nodded his head. "Yes. He was another member of the Resistance. I only met him a couple of times."

"So why did he want my papa to die? And why did he see him a month ago?" Lisi barely got the words across her dry lips.

"Papa wouldn't know that. Right, Papa?" Rose became defensive.

"Actually, Rose, I think I do." Mr. Meyer turned sad eyes to Lisi. "Your papa also had been part of the

Resistance, even before the War began. With your brother, Fritz." Lisi couldn't believe it. She was glad she already knew about Fritz, but her papa? And more surprising, her papa worked with Fritz? After how much he seemed to hate him? Fritz rarely came home to visit when they stationed him in Berlin before he was transferred to Austria, because of her papa. Even after he gained rank and was permitted to come home to visit more often, he rarely did. She knew this because of the letters he sent to her mama. She had read them. Every one. She knew where her mama hid them, even the ones that weren't addressed to the whole family.

Mr. Meyer knew this was a lot for Lisi to take in. He went on to explain. "That night of Kristallnacht, so long ago, some people from town found out about your papa and gave him a pretty good beating." Lisi remembered his leg. "But it didn't stop there. They continued to torture him for months until he finally caved."

Lisi shook her head. "No, you're wrong. My papa always hated the Nazi army. He would never give in and join them. Not even as a sympathizer. He was against them."

Mr. Meyer patted Lisi's arm. "I know this must be very difficult for you to understand, but what I tell you is the truth. Your papa was a very strong man, but he feared what the Nazis were capable of doing, not only to him but to...." His voice trailed off. He didn't need to finish his sentence. Lisi knew what Mr. Meyer meant. Her papa became a Nazi collaborator to protect his family. To protect her.

Mr. Meyer cleared his throat and continued. "Just know, Lisi, that your papa did a lot of good things when he was with us. After he left I still managed to keep an eye on him. I wanted to make sure nothing happened to him." Mr. Meyer looked down at his hands. "I guess I didn't do a very good job. The war ended, and I thought it was all over."

It didn't make sense. "What do you mean you thought 'it' was all over? What else aren't you telling me?"

"Lisi, my papa wouldn't keep anything from you. Right, Papa?" Lisi heard the doubt soaked in Rose's question.

Mr. Meyer looked at Rose, then to Lisi. "Lisi, I promise you I had no idea the Resistance would do this to your papa. He was a good man. I thought when I told the American Army about him that he would be protected."

Lisi felt her pulse quicken and thought she would pass out. "Tell me, please." Closing her eyes, she waited for the final curtain call.

"Not long after the war began your papa started suspecting a mole in our group." In response to the blank stares, he continued. "What I mean is, he believed that someone in our Resistance group was a Nazi spy. One night, I don't know how, but your papa found out who."

Lisi didn't need him to continue. She knew. "Von Gross."

"Yes. Of course, once exposed he had been thrown out of the group. Last we heard the Nazi army sent him to fight in Russia. Then the War ended and as I said, we thought it was over."

Lisi shook her head, squeezing her eyes shut to clear her brain. "So what you're telling me is that this Von Gross shot and killed my papa? And you thought that when the War ended it would all just vanish? My papa wasn't even part of the Resistance anymore!"

Mr. Meyer felt sorry. "I'm sorry Lisi. I can promise you that the American army has already captured him and he will pay for his crime."

Rose shook her head, still trying to come to grips with her papa's own role in all this. "Papa, all this time. What you taught us about respecting the Nazis. I...." Rose couldn't finish her sentence.

Mr. Meyer hung his head. "I'm so sorry, Rose. I was a coward. Yes, I acted as a Nazi sympathizer. I couldn't tell you. It would have put all of our lives in terrible danger. Please understand, I had to. I did it for you."

All this new information overwhelmed Lisi. She stood up and walked to the door.

"Lisi?" Mr. Meyer called to her. She looked at him, seeing double. "One more thing. Just because the war is over, obviously there are still strong feelings."

Lisi blinked to focus. She understood. Mumbling her thanks she headed home. She had to tell her mama. There was no way she could keep this a secret.

CHAPTER 40

The next month passed in a blur to Lisi. After telling her mama everything that had happened with Mr. Von Gross and Mr. Meyer, she still wasn't sure if that was the best decision. She had never seen her mama cry so much. They buried her papa and prepared for Christmas. Even in the midst of the sorrow, Lisi felt a peace. She had forgiven her papa. She felt sorry for him. She had never known the torture he must have had to endure to stand up for what he believed in. To her, it wasn't completely his fault that he became a Nazi collaborator. She only hoped that he returned to the truth before it was too late. Just like she did.

Christmas came and was a happy time even though it seemed strange to Lisi. She still wasn't used to not having her papa around, but the great thing was that Lea, Johann and Rille all came to stay with her and her mama for a week. Johann filled the evenings with stories of his time as a prisoner in France. Jerry spent that Christmas with her family, as well as the next one. He filled a small void and

"Where are who?" Rose asked. Mr. Archibault noticed how the few years since he and Lisi had last visited Rose hadn't been kind to her.

"Ruth and Peter. I'm assuming they moved and lost touch with you two since I've never known about them before."

"Peter moved back east to his old hometown. Ruth met a soldier and moved away, I think to England. We lost touch for a while until recently. Ruth's younger brother, Henry, still lived here and died of a heart attack a month ago. Ruth and Peter both returned for his funeral. Ruth decided to stay and help his wife for a while. She isn't dealing very well with Henry's death." Ruth looked down at the photograph she held in her hand. She couldn't believe after all these years the photograph Jerry took his last day in their town still survived. She looked up. "Would you like to meet her?"

Did he want to meet her? Mr. Archibault just found out his wife was a hero, and now he had the chance to meet the woman whose life she changed. "Of course, I want to meet her." He smiled at Rose.

She smiled back. "Good, because here she comes."

"Did I miss the story?" Mr. Archibault turned toward the sound of the gentle voice.

"Yes. You missed the whole thing," Rose replied smiling.

"I'm sorry. I couldn't get away any sooner. Hello, you must be Herr Archibault." Mr. Archibault took the extended hand and held it as he examined the woman standing in front of him. She was tall, even though her

199

shoulders slumped a little. Her chin-length white hair pulled back in a clip. Bright, blue eyes still sparkled as she spoke, revealing some of her youth that remained. Her English was excellent.

"Please, call me Jim. It's nice to finally meet you, Ruth. I've just learned a lot about you."

"All good things, I hope." Ruth gave a wink.

"I just finished telling Jim the story of how you and Lisi met, and how you helped each other." Rose moved over to let Ruth sit on the bench too. Then she handed her the photograph.

"Oh my gosh, I can't believe this photograph has survived the test of time." Ruth rubbed her wrinkled hand across the smooth faces. "I first met them in 1945. I don't know that I would say I helped Lisi as much as she helped me. Herr Archibault," Ruth paused, "Jim, your wife was a hero. In every sense of the word." Ruth paused again, and Mr. Archibault wondered how healthy this woman was. "I know she wanted to have a cause, do something great for the war effort. And she did, maybe not in the way she expected, but she sure did.

"We were different, the refugees. We spoke with different accents, some of us spoke different languages at first, and we looked different. But in the end, none of that mattered to Lisi. I know it was very difficult for her, to welcome me the way she did, but her bravery carried me through the worst times of my life. My whole family, really." Ruth paused again, and Mr. Archibault saw one tear trickle down her cheek. "I'm not sure how I would have survived if she didn't befriend me that year."

Mr. Archibault reached out and held the frail hand in his, and Rose held the other. The three of them sat there that day, on a special bench handcrafted by a man who probably lost his life during one of the worst times in history. A time when the evil truth was hidden for a short while behind a beautiful tapestry of lies.

TO THE READER

Lisi Hertz was a hero. While she didn't fight in World War II like her brothers, she was part of another Resistance. She put a very special friendship on the line to show kindness to someone different.

We don't need a war to be a hero and have a purpose. We can do the same. Every day we find ourselves surrounded by people who are bullied or ignored for being different. At school, sports, and in the community, we all have the chance to be heroes. Just like Lisi. It might take courage beyond what we believe we possess on our own, but if we trust in God's guidance and love, we can accomplish great feats.

AUTHOR'S NOTE

Lisi Hertz is a fictional character whose life is based on the real-life events of an incredible woman named Elisabeth. Elisabeth grew up in a small town in the heart of Germany during the reign of Hitler. According to Elisabeth, her family remained anti-Nazi during the war and refused to be swayed by neighbors. She had three older brothers, all of whom served in the war and were prisoners of war. All three returned home safely. She also had two older sisters.

Elisabeth was a little younger than Lisi, so many of the events during the war were fictional based on pieces from her memory. Lisi's friends were all fictional. The friendship between Lisi and Rose was based on the relationship between Lisi and her best friend. However, the estrangement between Lisi and Rose was purely fictional as was Rose's character as a Nazi sympathizer. Ruth's character was taken from the fact that Elisabeth remembered many refugee families who came to town and settled there.

Elisabeth's father had actually been taken to work for the American soldiers. He was involved in a car accident which caused permanent brain damage but did not kill him. Elisabeth and her father did not have a very good relationship.

Many of the events regarding the Resistance as well as what happened to Lea were not recorded events from Elisabeth. However, based on historical research and interviews, these events could have actually taken place.

Elisabeth met a young Canadian soldier, much more wonderful than Peter's character, named Joe. They met at a restaurant where she worked in Germany. They married, and Elisabeth eventually moved to the United States in 1959.

98390856R10115